I0738290

THE NOVA
PROJECT 70

THE NOVA
PROJECT 70

A Science Fiction Trilogy
Based on a screenplay by Fabion O. Reeves

BOOK I

Gregory Ross Miller
Fabion O. Reeves

Edited by Rachel Curry-Houston,
David Windsor, and William Miller.

ISBN: 978-0-578-54610-0

Library of Congress, Washington, DC

Subsidiary of Project 70 Publishing
Los Angeles, CA

Nova Painting by Fabion O. Reeves

* * * * *

Et In Terra Pax

* * * * *

"Look up at the stars
and not down at your feet.
Try to make sense of what you see
and wonder about what makes the
universe exist. Be curious."

Stephen William Hawking
1942 - 2018

<u>Acknowledgements</u>

To God from whom all blessings flow for allowing me to learn the three truths, while being there every step of the way; to my mother, Elouise Miller, for her tremendous love and affection; to my father, Walter Miller, for providing the mystery which fueled my thirst for knowledge; to my church, St. James in the City Episcopal Church (Los Angeles), for placing me on a path of righteousness and literary expansion; to Dorothy Papadakos, you are a wonderful inspiration; to Dr. Ronald Busuttil, M.D., Ph.D., for your 'Nobel' inspiration in providing me the most compelling start of this incredible journey…walking in the footsteps of Roman Frederick Starzl, a great science fiction writer; to Nina Bunche Pierce for helping me to discover who I am by allowing me to enter the world of her grandfather, Nobel Prize laureate Dr. Ralph J. Bunche; to Fabion Reeves, a very good creative writer, for providing the foundation for this epic story to be written and for keeping me on my feet throughout the prelude as we now embark upon the complexities of the fugue; to all my instructors from P. S. 90 (Harlem), Beekman Hill International School, Riverdale Country School, Touro College (NYC), and Harvard University, you're all fantastic; to J. S. Bach, for composing the music that lives within me; this chapter in my life will be nothing short of remarkable.

Los Angeles, California

21 March 2018

First, I'd like to thank my grandmother, Rebertha Miller –Reeves, for housing me while I wrote the Nova screenplay. Secondly, I'd like to thank my mother, Marlene Stewart, and my father, Everdeen Reeves, for giving me the genes to make life's necessary tasks possible. Since a person is nothing without the environment, I thank the people who continuously nourish me in my surroundings, whatever the conditions may be. I want to thank all my teachers throughout life for finding ways to get me to read and write when I did not understand. Thank God for mathematically connecting me with Gregory Ross Miller, who walked me through this entire project and whom I look forward to working with on many other projects. Most importantly, I'd like to thank the almighty God, who has given me life to accomplish, we thank thee, God, we thank thee!

Los Angeles, California
21 March 2018

Fabion O. Reeves

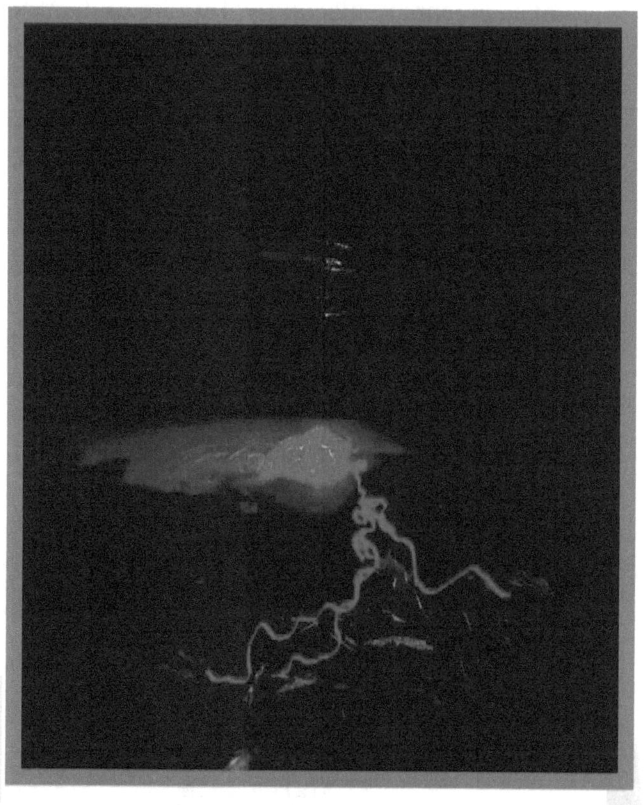

The Nova (novaerium)

Painting by Fabion O. Reeves

"There was a huge brightness from the flames as Mark looked down into the crater's core and noticed an iridescent neon purple liquid bleeding out from its center."

CONTENTS

CHAPTER 1   Praeludium...................................13

CHAPTER 2   Strange Encounter......................... 19

CHAPTER 3   The Return Home 37

CHAPTER 4   Vivat Rex! 45

CHAPTER 5   Looking Back 53

CHAPTER 6   Blown Away..................................69

CHAPTER 7   Emergency 79

CHAPTER 8   The Interrogation 92

CHAPTER 9   The Hidden Secret 102

CHAPTER 10   Think It, It Does It............................117

CHAPTER 11   Abduction 124

CHAPTER 12   Run for Cover 143

CHAPTER 13   13 Sarcophagi Red Tubes.................158

CHAPTER 14   Search and Destroy 180

CHAPTER 15   Unexpected Guests 204

CHAPTER 16   Destination Mars............................. 216

CHAPTER 17   A Gift from a Goddess......................228

In the beginning, God created the heavens and the Earth. And the Earth was without form and empty, and darkness was on the face of the Earth, and the Spirit of God hovered over the face of the universe. Then God looked down upon the Earth and said, let there be light… and there was light. **Genesis 1:1-3**

And God will give you the power to grow and you will venture beyond this world and thereafter God will return you to it in death, and then He will bring you forth from it in the resurrection.

And God has made many spaces so that you might have the freedom to choose your future on a more spacious path.

CHAPTER 1

PRAELUDIUM

The year is 2060 and we are living in a solar system filled with illuminated interstellar objects. On any given night over the Florida peninsula one can see, with the common eye, planets, stars, satellites, the space station, and even space shuttles loaded with passengers entering and exiting our orbit.

For the record, these bright celestial bodies occupy merely a small fragment of the Milky Way galaxy. During it all, our beautiful blue planet Earth floats within the Orion arm of the Milky Way, which lies about two-thirds of the way out from the centre of the galaxy. Named for the Orion constellation, the Orion Arm is one of the most remarkable constellations of the northern hemisphere winter night sky.

To summarize this, some of the illustrious stars and most prominent celestial objects of this constellation, Betelgeuse, Rigel, the stars of Orion's Belt, the Orion Nebula, are positioned within the Orion Arm. It is the place where most of the gas and dust clouds are located. It is also where astronomical events cause the spectacular appearances of bright new stars. This is also the birthplace of Polaris, a brilliant star, and other relatively known and unknown bright stars.

But in the same way the Earth has an equator, so too does the Milky Way, which is a spiral galaxy measuring 100,000 light-years across and only 1,000 light-years thick. To gain a visual perspective of this one must imagine a compact disc spinning in the hard drive of their computer, yet instead of being made of polycarbonate, aluminium, plastic, and lacquer, it is composed of stars.

The galactic equator is the halfway point between the top and bottom of that disk and we are about fourteen light years above what is called the equatorial symmetry plane.

In addition, the five brightest planets in Earth's solar system, Mercury, Venus, Mars, Jupiter, and Saturn - have all been known since ancient times and can easily be seen with the common eye if one knows where and when to look for them. They are visible for much of the year, except for short periods of time when they are too close to the Sun to observe, however, with the use of powerful telescopes, a person can take on a much vaster realm of the galaxy. Occasionally, the planet Venus, more than any of these five planets, prominently illuminates the evening sky over Southern Florida, outshining all the stars in the vicinity, including Sirius, a solar system which has the reputation of being the brightest visible star in the Earth's night sky.

But let's talk about the universe. According to our knowledge of cosmology, the universe was featureless and dark for quite a long time. The first stars did not appear until millions of years after the big bang and nearly one billion years passed before galaxies extended across the cosmos.

Astronomers have long wondered how this dramatic transition from darkness to light came about. However, while our goal is not to profoundly explain the algorithm of the universe, I'm afraid this is something you'll have to research independently.

Meteorites or falling stars as they are known to the common man are only a fragment of the interesting makeup of our solar system.

With the ability to look through powerful telescopes in observatories across our planet, we're able to view thousands of illuminated objects darting across the sky like flagellum racing to fertilize an ovum. However, asteroids were everywhere and at any given moment one would burst across the sky and collide into the Earth.

At any rate, it is a little-known fact that alterations within the cosmology of these planets result in climate changes, which affect the ecology and environment of our planet even though the Earth was blessed with a plenitude of natural resources.

Scientists are currently working on various experiments to find how this affects us and what can be done to safeguard the ecosystem already in place for future generations. We must understand that what we do here on Earth affects the future of all the other planets in our solar system and beyond.

But today, we are experiencing drastic changes in the environment. For instance, at one-time Florida had over three thousand miles of coastline whose extremes extended from the tropical to the warm temperate zones.

These have all but changed drastically over decades. Natural physical forces created by shifts in moons surrounding neighbouring planets have created barrier islands and offshore keys which once had abundant shallow quiet waters, but now these have all but disappeared.

This is evidence of changes in the deep ecology of the environment.

It had already been predicted not long ago that seas would rise 78.74 centimetres by 2060 and this has been proven to be exact. Fishing, which at one time had been abundant, has now all but disappeared.

Subsequently, seagrass beds that used to be nurseries and feeding grounds for young fish and shrimp have all but disappeared. You may then ask the question, "Why are the sharks in such abundance still?"

Disregarding the ever-increasing rise in shark population, people continue to pack the beaches to bathe in the warm waters of the Atlantic Ocean.

But this is not a story about water, beaches, sharks, or swimming. This is the story of General Mark William George Parker, United States Special Operations Officer, former United States Air Force high speed reconnaissance aircraft pilot, mechanical engineer, owner of a sports bar and grill, which houses an underground mechanical engineering laboratory where he would develop, build, and test mechanical devices such as engines and tools. It was here that he originally created the blueprint of a vehicle called 'The Machine.'

This is also the place where he developed and engineered many machine designs, fabrications, robotics, energy creation and control, constructed prototypes; overseeing the production and manufacturing of the final product, spending lots of time around dangerous tools and occasionally using hazardous chemicals in his laboratory.

This story is about the homecoming of a man who just arrived back from a secret mission called *Project 70*, a high-level intelligence venture between British aristocrats and the elite organizers of the third coming of the Continental Congress.

This is the story of a strange encounter which occurred during this mission which left Mark with a mutation that enabled him to acquire super-human powers with the ability to think and solve equations that have baffled scientists over the years. This is the story of the *Nova*.

CHAPTER 2

2050 STRANGE ENCOUNTER

ur story begins eight thousand miles away in a military hideout, deep in the coniferous forest surrounding the mountains of Nanga Parbat. It was during the early morning hours of November 14, 2050, that a giant meteorite entered the atmosphere and fell capriciously towards Earth.

But before we get deep into our story, let me give you some information that might help paint a picture. Up until global warming, the mountains would be covered with snowfall this time of year, however; nowadays you would think it were summer with the landscape totally green.

Furthermore, Nanga Parbat lies in a mysterious environment and the mountain, which is the ninth highest in the world and the second highest peak in Pakistan, has a terrible reputation. It stands 8,126 meters above sea level, its peak rising in forbidden solitude more than 6,706 meters above the dreary land of the Indus Valley at the western end of the Himalayas. That puts it about Mount Everest, Earth's greatest mountain. Notoriously known as the Killer Mountain, this giant behemoth once took a toll on sixteen human lives (seven climbers and nine high porters) at one time.

It is also known as Naked Mountain and legend has it that when the sun sets, it smokes up there. They even say that red dragons live in its mountainous caves and breathe fire and blow smoke through their huge nostrils thus allowing fairies to cook their bread. These are presumably local legends, paradoxically, they may extend beyond the realm of just mere fantasy.

Prior to the fiery meteorite falling, Mark and his team arrived in the early morning hours by a stealth military quadcopter and were air dropped with supplies about 1.7 kilometres from the vicinity of the secured military base camp. Subsequently, they made the short but treacherous journey along a labyrinth of passages to their designated location.

Upon arrival, Mark inspected the grounds and discovered an old matte grey and green 4 x 4 military jeep. He inspected the vehicle's body and found that it sustained very little weather damage; maybe a few scratches here and there, no major rusting and the tires looked sturdy. *That's all that mattered* he thought.

He opened the door to the cabin, went inside and inspected the glove compartment. He came across a small camouflage covered canteen and a green tin box which he opened. There he found a silver key lying flat on a bed of polyurethane foam that looked as if it might fit into the ignition of the vehicle. He took the key and inserted it. After several attempts, he was finally able to start the engine. He was amazed that the vehicle was still functional. The slightly rusted fuel level gauge indicated that there were at least three-quarters of a tank of gas inside - more than enough to navigate the area.

He shook the canteen and found that it was half filled with some sort of fluid. He screwed off the top and put it to his nose. It smelled like vodka. He poured a little on the tip of his finger. It certainly tasted like vodka, a little stale but still able to satisfy ones craving for a stiff hard drink. He held the canteen to his mouth and took a sip. The harsh taste made him grimace and cough a few times. He wiped his mouth, screwed the top back on the canteen, and placed it in the right leg pocket of his green and tan combat fatigue trousers.

*　*　*　*　*

It didn't take long for Mark and his men to complete setting up their intelligence camp. Their mission was to eliminate terrorism and restore peace and tranquillity throughout the world. And here in these majestic mountains and their surrounding territories is where it will all begin.

As the afternoon quickly faded, evening slowly descended upon the Earth even though the blackness of night was still hours away. However, after taking in a hot meal, a few drinks amidst great storytelling around a crackling fire, the men decided to retire to their canvas army tents, all except Mark. Somewhat of a soothsayer, upon arrival, he sensed something eerie about the geology of this great mountain. He gathered from geological source illustrations that during the early morning hours the foothills of Nanga Parbat appeared somewhat achromatic. They rarely produced this much dense fog and precipitated mist, especially at this hour.

However, today he noticed the ghost grey fog was overwhelmingly thick. With this much smoke, you would think the mountain's base was in the lair of a great fire-breathing dragon whose propensity was to do nothing more but sleep and snore during the day and growl, hiss, and blow smoke rings through its nostrils at night.

This same terrifying beast would then take to flight, traveling long distances with its powerful leathery wings, before swooping down on sleeping villagers in neighboring towns, knocking down their houses, roasting those who couldn't escape by breathing fire upon them, gathering their burnt bodies with its huge talons and carrying them off to its lair to feed its hungry young.

* * * * *

Mark had a creative imagination and was the last to relax after his men had called it a night. Their mission was to rise early and begin tracking the most wanted terrorists on Earth until they found them. Afterwards, their orders were to capture them and bring their prisoners in to higher authorities to face justice. Even though Nanga Parbat would be their starting point, this mission would take them to some of the most remote places on the face of the Earth.

* * * * *

I'm glad this day is over, Mark thought to himself as he relaxed, chewing on a piece of dried emu jerky, and taking a swig of the slightly stale vodka. He had a habit of thinking to himself and so it didn't seem to bother him at all. Quite often he found himself soliloquizing and always thought it was a healthful way of clearing one's head while collecting one's thoughts.

However, the thing is he always made sure that it wasn't conspicuous. He didn't want anyone to think he was going mad, even though this desolate and murky landscape was enough to make anyone forget his or her faculties.

* * * * *

Mark took another swig of the vodka and settled down and reminisced back to when he was a child in school. He remembered a poem from a book he had read back then and began to recite it. As he gazed up into the stars, he began soliloquizing the poem.

Over the mountains grey and dreary,
In dungeons wet, cold, and weary,
Red dragons sleep, their mood is eerie,
Their eyes look up, yet they are bleary,

The mountains rise beneath the moon,
The dragon trampers the thought of doom,
It fled its lair amidst the gloom,
A horde of treasures in its room,

Over the mountains dark and dreary,
In dungeons wet, cold, and weary,
Red dragons sleep, their mood is eerie,
They wait till night; their steps are leery.

Mark couldn't help but beam a little and was quite surprised that he remembered the poem he learned many years ago when he attended prep school back in Henley, a small city in the United Kingdom. He remembered how he would always imagine a fierce red dragon in its lair and always said to himself that one day he would embark upon a journey that would take him to a faraway land, maybe a distant unknown planet, where red dragons ruled a strange yet enchanted world.

He always said to himself that even though dragons had terrible reputations, his goal was to capture one, tame it, and become its friend. He thought about this and many other fantasies, but he quickly changed his thoughts because he didn't want to become distracted from the real purpose of this mission.

Regardless of the many thoughts that were simultaneously racing through his head, the most important was to catch and eliminate terrorists in the area, and tops on the list were those associated with the curse of Elanor Annadurai, which folklore states that one who was cursed by this fiendish outlaw would be ostracized to the remote areas of Siberia to live among the Yeti and other mythical beasts that supposedly inhabited the frozen tundra. The only way one could break this curse was to exercise terrorism thus bringing the probability of doom to all mankind. It was for this purpose that Mark was determined that he and his men would take on this special hi-level mission and accomplish this task. You see, he had a stubborn temperament and his goal was to stay focused and on top of the most important details of his life.

He often found himself solving complex mathematical equations and coming up with solutions to problems that others never had the courage to wrestle with, but nevertheless, he was determined, courageous, a leader, extremely humble, and creative plus he held on to his morals, his dreams, and most importantly, his faith in God. He patterned his life after Saint Mark the Evangelist who is the ascribed author of the Gospel of Mark.

Even though this is where his purpose in life stemmed, he would often find himself saying things like "My God, what am I doing here and why am I not someplace sitting home with a wife and kids and working a nine to five?"

He would then answer his own questions. Hypothetically speaking, he always thought he was the most complex soliloquizer on the planet.

* * * * *

As he sat in his warm tent going over his plans and pondering his upcoming assignment, he noticed how peaceful things were. He looked up at the sky through the transparent roof of his tent and saw a full moon which illuminated the Earth as if it were the break of dawn. He looked out through the entrance of the tent and examined the landscape.

He noticed much of the area around the base of the mountain consisted of alpine meadows, covered with lush wild grasses and colourful wildflowers. Beyond and around them were great peaks covered by dense pine forests, tall spruce, and fir trees, giving the appearance as if one were in the Caucasus Mountains instead of the Himalayas, but then again, they have their similarities. *I could go for this type of peace and tranquillity back home in Florida* he thought as he looked up at the bright, vibrant full moon.

*   *   *   *   *

As night quickened, the silhouettes of the evergreen trees that populated the base of the foothills came to resemble the tall-spired minarets of the Süleymaniye_Mosque in Turkey where great barn owls would perch themselves high upon the branches overseeing the meadows below and call out into the wilderness.

Nonetheless, Mark continued to enjoy the quiet evening, when suddenly, he heard a rustling in the bush not far from his tent. He quickly reached for his military neuro-disruptor 45 and prepared to shoot the invader.

"These critters seem to want to come out and play at night more so than during the day," he quietly said to himself.

Wildlife was far from scarce up in the mountains. There were several bird breeds and folklore talked about giant elga birds, large enough to swoop down and pick up a man with their talons and carry him off to a nest of hungry younglings, waiting to devour him, leaving nothing but skull and bones.

Mark checked the digital display on his neuro-disruptor to make sure it was loaded just in case he had to use it.

"If one of these critters even tries jumping out at me, I'll destroy it," he implied.

He had no idea what type of critter was in the bushes, it may not even be a critter, but then again, perhaps it may be a marmot or something smaller, and hopefully not a snow leopard. He heard stories about the Markhor, Himalayan brown bear, musk deer, lynx, and Kashmir grey langur, but he knew that they were all extinct, if not on the brink of extinction.

He looked at his watch. It was almost midnight and the members of his platoon were already fast asleep. Mark ignored the critter that was making the noise in the bushes. Without warning, it stuck its little head out. It was the smallest deer he had ever seen. *There must be an elven village nearby* he thought. Mark smiled and tried to coax the small creature to come closer. He grabbed a handful of foliage and reached out hoping that it would eat from his hand.

"Come here little wide-eyed beauty. I have something for you."

The creature only stared at Mark momentarily before springing back into the woods.

"If there are more of you around then it's safe because you guys don't bother anybody and besides, all you eat is foliage and I'm meat. You don't want me," he assured himself.

*　*　*　*　*

It was getting late and Mark was getting tired of thinking. He wanted to rest. He took a chance to lie down for a bit. He hated to do so because his mind would start to wander, and he would become stressed just thinking about all the things he had to do. He thought what would happen after he completes this heroic duty for his country. He also thought how he would be rewarded with a medal of honour and a ticker tape parade. Occasionally, he would look at a picture of the world's most notorious terrorist he carried in his wallet. He would then think to himself how he would never forget this guy and always wanted to remember his face just in case he ever happened to come across him. You would have thought Mark had a personal vendetta against him; but it was his job to protect and serve his country and the world.

Eventually, Mark let out a huge yawn and started to become very tired. *I need to lie down* he thought to himself; and so, he did just that. No sooner than he shut his eyes he opened them again, looked up into the black starlit sky and saw a huge radiant meteorite, perhaps a fireball of some sort he thought but no, even larger, a superbolide entering Earth's atmosphere, streaking across the mountains. He observed the object and immediately jumped up with astonishment and ran out of his tent. The descending object was quite bright as it streaked across the blackened sky, leaving an iridescent trail of brilliant lights and sparkles. It appeared more than just a mysterious light whizzing past and was accompanied by the sound of multiple, powerful blasts.

Amazing, he thought. *I need to investigate this further.*

He then ran towards the abandoned jeep, jumped inside and quickly started it, turned on the headlights and drove in the direction where he thought the meteorite might have fallen. Despite the powerful noise the projectile made as it swooped across the sky, Mark never heard the actual crash into the Earth. This was an indication that it might have fallen quite some distance away. Nonetheless, he was determined to find it. He drove as fast as he could, which was difficult considering it was night and the unpredictable terrain was extremely rugged with tree branches and vines that webbed the ground in some places. He had to cross a narrow tributary which stemmed from the Indus River but luckily for him the jeep was built to sustain this type of driving. As he drove, he noticed a cloud of red dust and that the terrain was torn as if a vortex tornado had passed through the area. He also noticed a ghastly illumination throughout the mist. Suddenly, Mark came to where the meteorite had fallen. He stopped within a few centimeters from the site and turned on the vehicles floodlights.

Right away, he pulled up the location information on his forearm device, which indicated he was near a wooded plateau called *Novaerwuld*, a place known for its powerful wind turbulence, and storm unpredictability, 35° 14' 9.00" North latitude by 74° 35' 12.59" East longitude.

He went out and cautiously walked towards the point of impact. There was a huge crater in the ground; about 1,945 meters in diameter and 197 meters in depth and flames were coming out from it. In front of the crater, there was a burning bush, which appeared to be lit by fire but not actually burning. It had a purplish glow, which Mark found to be quite strange. He quickly made his way around this bush and continued toward the crater's edge. The meteorite was embedded deep in the sunken hole. There was a huge brightness from the flames and Mark looked down into the crater's core and noticed an iridescent neon purple liquid bleeding out from its centre.

This is strange he thought as he cautiously proceeded towards the object. He moved closer to the edge of the crater and amid the torrid heat, he noticed a purple mist rising from within, perhaps because of it cooling and becoming accustomed to the surrounding temperature.

As it cooled, the fusion crust of the giant metallic meteorite began to ablate as if something were inside attempting to break out of a confined space. Nevertheless, Mark became anxious to examine the substance closer and searched around for a probing device. There were plenty of long and sturdy branches still on uprooted birch trees because of the object's impact. He grabbed the nearest one and broke off a piece. It must have been at least 2 meters long and sturdy. It even had a tip that was naturally designed like a small spoon.

In the meantime, Mark allowed the object to cool for about an hour. It was still dark, maybe a little past one in the morning. He searched for something to contain a sample but all he had was his canteen with a little vodka left inside. He immediately opened the canteen and drank the remaining vodka, thus emptying it completely. It wasn't much and so he had no worries about getting intoxicated and maybe driving into a ditch, not being able to find his way back to base camp. He looked around for something to wash and dry the interior but there was nothing to be found. He then remembered crossing the small tributary and accessed his vehicle and drove back to find it.

When he arrived, he filled the canteen with cool water, tossed it around inside for a bit and then poured it out. He then refilled it and drove back to the crater. There he shook the container and poured out the remaining water.

He then ripped off a small piece of his shirt and wrapped it around the tip of a twig. He pushed the cloth covered twig into the mouth of the canteen and dried the insides completely.

Afterwards, he looked in the back of the vehicle and found a medium-sized black duffle bag with mountaineer equipment inside. There was a climbing harness, a locking carabiner device, an LED headlamp, gloves, and a reel of kernmantle rope. There was even a pair of adjustable spiked crampon slippers that he carefully slipped over his rugged boots, thus giving him the ability to secure his footage as he climbed. He put on the harness and immediately tied a figure eight. He anchored the locking device to the toll hook. He then grabbed his stick and canteen and walked awkwardly towards the crater's edge.

The torrid heat raged out from the object, yet Mark continued to slowly make his way down into the abyss, securing each footstep by grasping the sides of the crater with his spiked boots. Carefully, he descended its depths until he was within 1.2 meters of the object. The smell exuded from the meteorite was metallic with a higher scent of lavender. It was hot down there and Mark was sweating profusely.

He took his hand and wiped away the sweat which poured down his face and didn't want it to drip into his eyes for fear of being temporarily blinded. He then reached out with the probing device to obtain a small sample of the purple fluid oozing from its core. He carefully placed the sample into the canteen, screwed on the top and secured it into his left leg pocket with a Velcro flap.

As he finished gathering the sample, without warning, a thick gaseous bubble burst from within the meteorite, quickly releasing a small precipitation of the fluid into the air which landed on his right forearm immediately leaving a bleached spot. He gasped, released the probing device, and almost losing control while twirling around numerous times before nearly falling off his harness into the crater.

As he grabbed hold of the harness with his other hand, he noticed that there was inflammation exponentially increasing on the injured arm. He tried wiping the substance away onto his pants, but it immediately began to lacerate his skin exposing what appeared to be the epidermis level. Unable to sustain the pain any longer he cried out into the wilderness as the fluid penetrated his body. He wiped the sweat from his face and gasped in horror as he attempted to reject the fear that this ordeal could possibly mutate him into some horribly disfigured creature, and never again would he be able to work or appear in public. He quickly made his way up to the top of the crater and crawled out onto the ground. He sat motionless for a few seconds to catch his breath before slowly standing up, realizing then that he was feeling quite awful.

As he continued to wipe away the substance, little was he aware that an alien chemical, known only to the inhabitants of Mars, had already begun to permeate his bloodstream. This would later cause the mutation that would remain with him throughout his entire life. He felt an excruciating pain and his body slowly started to shut down as he became weaker.

He didn't know if he would be able to make it safely back to camp. As he looked deep into his mind's eye, he wondered why this happened, and could only realize that right now he was alone in the wilderness, but for how long?

Could this déjà vu be a replication of Jesus' journey of forty days and forty nights spent out in the wilderness being tempted by Satan? As much as he tried to clear up the confusion in his mind, he knew he must focus on attempting to make it back to camp before anything else occurred. He asked himself *why did he go chasing after that meteorite*? Was it temptation that drove him away from his men and his mission? Was this to be his fate? And what if this fate led him down a darker path? Will he be doomed to die in a dismal land where ravens would pluck out his eyes, vultures would eat away at his flesh and squirrels would gnaw away at his bones? Why did he allow himself to be led astray chasing this foreign object into the darkness? What type of control did this meteorite have over him?

He saw a bright light and heard heavy footsteps, crushing leaves and rushing towards him. He became afraid and didn't know what to think. Could this be a creature that came out of the object, perhaps a Martian on its way to capture him and take him back into space as a prisoner to the forbidden red planet from once it came?

Mark tried to cry out for help but was too weak to neither utter a word nor move his body as the toxic purple chemical slowly drained him of all his strength. What made matters worse was his fear of the onslaught of danger coming from an unknown assailant, with a brightly lighted object of some sort that presented the possibility of bodily harm or even death. He became so frightened that his heart began to palpitate, and he found himself gasping for air.

As the light became brighter and the footsteps quickened, growing louder with every step gained, Mark's head became clouded with ominous thoughts. Suddenly, he began to panic, then without warning, he collapsed and fell unconscious to the ground.

CHAPTER 3

2060 THE RETURN HOME

s morning arrived temperatures soared high and automated sprinkler systems cooled the environment. Global warming had reached a point where temperatures were greater than usual this time of year, but they were still tolerable to most. It was going to be an extremely warm and sunny St. Patrick's Day in Miami, Florida and in just a matter of time beaches would be packed with people, basking in the sand and swimming in the warm waters off the coast.

It was 5:30 in the morning and the crew at Mark's secluded sports bar and grill were preparing for the regular early morning diners to arrive. It was a Monday and the diner, known for its exquisite cuisine, had just received an ample supply of international food products from the world market over at 45 Mar Largo Street.

Meghan Reynolds, a beautiful former actress with the face of an angel, not only worked at the diner but was also the girlfriend of Mark, who would be arriving home today from his mission. Meghan was lovely by all standards and her flaxen hair accented her sparkling sapphire eyes. She was tall enough to once have been considered for a modeling contract with the top agency in Florida. She was anxious to see Mark again and her anticipation was evident. She was quite nervous, and it was obvious to the regulars who undoubtedly noticed the spilling of coffee, well maybe a cup or two, but nevertheless, she continued to give customers quality service with a smile. She knew that her life was about to change, and she had to accept it.

Running the diner for ten years while Mark was away wasn't easy, nevertheless, it didn't take long for Meghan to learn. She often found life to be a lonely existence, especially after leaving work, not having a social life she usually found herself heading straight home to the quiet neighbourhood of Riverdale, where she lived in a beautiful two-story red brick house on St. James Street. The house was surrounded by a lovely garden of laburnums, various follies, red trilliums, wild geraniums, white lilies, and flowering strelitzia reginae, offset by small palms, Spanish chestnut and birch trees. The sides and exterior gardens had sprawling spruce and other pine trees accented by various fruit trees. There was a beautiful Italian marble waterfall that accented the garden. The water from it bounced down against the marble and then flowed quietly; this added a sense of peace and natural tranquillity to the home; alongside the occasional ribbitting of frogs, the chirping of crickets and the songs of wild birds. This house was a gift to Mark from his father, James, an architect known for designing numerous public and private administrative and cultural buildings, mansions for the rich, the university gardens, including this lovely house.

*　*　*　*　*

During his absence, Mark thought it would be a good idea to get a pet for Meghan and so three years ago he did. While on a mission in Brussels he purchased an Afghan hound and had it sent to her as a birthday present. It was a handsome pet that Meghan named *Vivat Rex*, but she settled for calling him Rex for short. She knew that having a pet would not only offer protection but also add vibrant life to the dreary days that she spent alone.

It didn't take long for the restaurant to become busy with people on their way to work. Their chattering amongst one another along with the clatter of pots and pans from the kitchen, the clinking of cutlery against melamine plates sitting atop glass tables turned the eatery into a noise maker's paradise. She had already served five customers and was tipped quite well, but the tips didn't matter much to her. She usually filled in waiting on tables when the place became busy and even though she was the owner's girlfriend, she didn't mind filling in to help make the business run more efficiently. It was clear that she wanted Mark to be pleased when he returned home.

The morning was progressing and after serving one of the regular customers, she noticed a call coming through on her hologram forearm device though she had it on silent, not wanting to disturb the diners. She glanced over at the clock and saw that it was 8:20 AM to be exact.

I can't believe how quickly time flies; it'll be noon before long she thought to herself. She was so immersed in the time that she forgot her device was still ringing. She quickly unfolded it and attempted to access its hologram display, but it discontinued right at that very moment. She noticed the name on the digital display indicated it was Domonic Parker, Mark's younger brother, who was calling. Right away she knew it was time to leave to go pick Mark up from the airport. She wouldn't be late for anything in the world and besides, she thought it would be best to leave early enough to avoid any traffic altercations along the way.

She called out to a waitress standing nearby.

"I have to leave and take care of a business matter; can you cover for me?"

The waitress smiled and assured Meghan that she would keep everything under control until her return.

It didn't take long for Meghan to put on a sweater and leave the diner. In the process, she activated the vehicle startup control from her forearm device, accessed her car and drove the distance towards the general airport. While driving, the automated voice asked if she wanted to switch to autonomous drive. Considering this, Meghan decided to continue to self-drive. She wanted to experience the freedom of self-driving if she could. She was aware that the world had changed, and robotics had gained tremendously in the race to defeat mankind, so she tried to always keep the human factor alive.

As she sped away, her device started to beep. She noticed through the car's digital system on the dashboard that it was Domonic calling again. This time she decided to answer it. She pressed a button on the steering wheel which activated the blue-tooth feature on her device.

"Hey Domonic, I just saw your missed call and was about to call you back. How is everything? Have you arrived in town?"

"Hi Meghan, all is well here. There was nothing major, as a matter of fact, it was a very comfortable ride and we just arrived at the rail terminal in Ft. Lauderdale, so I should see you all real soon. By the way, has Mark arrived yet?"

"No, I'm currently on the way to pick him up from the airport. The flight should be touching down shortly and I'm running late. You know how I dislike being late. I can't wait to see you Domonic."

"Sounds great Meg; listen, drive safely and we'll see you both tomorrow morning."

"Thanks, Domonic, we'll talk with you later."

*　*　*　*　*

Meghan was anxious to see Mark after all these years. As she pulled up and stopped in front of Terminal 6, she exited her vehicle, programmed it to automated valet, and proceeded to the waiting area. The terminal was quite busy with people traveling, but she was able to spot Mark sitting and removing his digital scroll from his forearm device. She noticed that he must have been working out because he appeared to be quite fit. She found this to be interesting since she's never seen him with this much muscle, and it excited her. Mark usually wore a military-style fade, which was sort of his trademark, but now his hair was shaven clean, and Meghan found this to be appealing as well. Also, what was unusual about his appearance was that he wore beige khaki military pants and a white cotton dress shirt opened at the neck, minus a tie. She found this to be peculiar as he always had a flair for high fashion, preferring British suits over Italian and would never be seen this casual ever.

As he looked up, he noticed Meghan staring and smiling at him. He rose from his seat and walked quickly towards her. She stretched out her arms to greet him and it didn't take long for them to lock in a romantic embrace.

It had been ten years since they were able to experience the freedom of being together like this and they both wanted to take advantage of the moment. There was nothing in this world that he loved more than his Meghan. Mark often thought about this moment but couldn't fully visualize how fantastic it would feel to be back in her arms again.

"I miss you so much," she sighed with relief. Tears fell from her eyes as he tenderly wiped them away.

"It's hard to understand the patience involved in waiting for a loved one to return from anywhere. I missed you and am so happy you're back," Meghan sighed.

Again, Mark wiped the tears from her face.

"I've been waiting forever for this moment to arrive. Let's go home."

Mark went over to the baggage carousel to retrieve his luggage; afterwards, he and Meghan quickly left the baggage area and made their way towards the exit. Meghan had already pre-programmed her vehicle to return to the terminal passenger loading area and she glimpsed at the map on her forearm device to confirm its arrival time.

"Our vehicle should be pulling around now."

Meghan turned back to face him, keeping her head down to peer up at him in a coquettish way. At that moment the automated vehicle arrived. It stopped in front of the terminal and the rear automatically opened allowing Mark to place his luggage in the trunk of the vehicle.

"I don't ever want you to leave me again," Meghan said as they embraced and kissed.

They both smiled and accessed the vehicle. Before they drove off, Mark investigated the rear-view mirror and noticed a green vehicle, the type driven by special military universal intelligence officers (UIO) parked off in the distance of about 0.2 kilometres away. It was turned backwards, and he could clearly see that the number forty-five was embedded across the trunk in big bold white numbers. There was almost something ominous about this green military vehicle and its relative number forty-five, but he couldn't put his hands on where he may have significantly seen it or why the number forty-five was so profound to him.

CHAPTER 4

VIVAT REX!

The drive home was nothing short of spectacular, a great feeling and more than anything Mark could have ever hoped for in the world. The opportunity to be back with Meghan lifted his spirit. It was obvious that they were both in love. Among other things, Mark was thankful for his sustaining faith in God and for having the virtue of patience, which was important to him while away on his mission. Furthermore, it wasn't easy being away all these years, not being able to communicate with those close to him, but this is what the government demanded as a security precaution. Hence, it was as if this secret high-level mission had taken away a little of his momentum but being back with the one he loved has helped to reinforce all of what was taken away.

"Where did you get this beautiful tungsten finished machine from?" he asked amusingly.

"Oh please, you know better than I."

He turned to Meghan and smiled.

"You look handsome with your shaven head," she admitted as she quickly took one hand off the steering wheel and rubbed his head. He squirmed like a child then threw her a kiss.

"Nice try, but is that the best you can do after being gone all these years?"

Mark smiled and shook his head. He was not used to such sarcasm coming from his lady but then again, he hadn't seen her in years and knew he owed her more than just a simulated sign of affection.

"You have to come better than that or else I'm going to take you back and drop you off where I picked you up."

Mark looked puzzled but knew she was being sarcastic, yet paradoxically, he sensed that she was serious. They both caught each other's eyes and laughed as she continued to drive down the winding road towards home.

"This was a very difficult and dangerous mission for me, and I wouldn't wish it on my worst enemy."

Meghan glanced over at Mark and smiled. She then quickly turned back towards the road and focused on the drive home. Simultaneously, she thought about several tasks on her to do list that she hadn't completed yet like cleaning up the boxes in the basement. She knew that if she left them scattered all over the place that sooner or later rats would find their way down there and build their nest in those boxes. But outside of that, not only did she want to get Mark back in the saddle; she also wanted to make sure that he was comfortable as well. She pressed a command on the steering wheel which prompted soft music to play. It was classical music and it was Mark's favourite type. He was fond of Bach, Widor, and Rachmaninoff and particularly loved the latter's second piano concerto.

"What did you miss most about me when I was away?" he asked looking out onto the unending acres of green pastures on both sides of the road. She pondered the question for a moment before answering.

"Well for one, I miss those funny little freckles that seem to dance whenever you smile," she said sarcastically.

"No, seriously, it seems like life is like a road that takes us across bridges and separates us, yet it brings us back together as well," she said as she reflected on those ten years of loneliness. She then continued looking out on the sides of the road.

"It takes you past churches, farms, homes, bodies of water, people, towns.... all of this is good, but it makes you realize how lonely life can be, especially when the one you love and want to be with is not there by your side." She then continued.

"I missed all of you. You see it's not easy expressing your thoughts to yourself and not having anyone to listen because you don't know who to trust or who would understand."

This reassured Mark of her love for him and made him smile. He gently reached for her hand and held it for a moment as she quickly released his hold so that she could have both hands on the steering wheel to safely focus on her driving.

"Yeah, it's peaceful and at the same time beautiful and I'm glad I'm back to enjoy it with you."

Meghan smiled as she continued to drive.

"Your brother just arrived in town from Los Angeles. He called as I was on my way to pick you up."

"Well, he better find a place to relax because I don't want to see him or anyone else until you and I spend a few days together, alone."

This brought a smile to Meghan's face. Her blue eyes sparkled, and it was obvious that she was the happiest girl in the world.

*　*　*　*　*

As Mark sat back listening to the quiet music, he focused on the ride home. He anticipated being able to resume his life like a normal person without any interference from the government, his brother, or anyone else for that matter. His thoughts were only on Meghan, as well as his independence, his vehicles, his business, and his other prospects. That's all that mattered to him now that he was no longer bonded by government rules and regulations and chasing terrorists around the world.

As they drove, they approached a railroad crossing at a fork in the road right before the barrier arms came down to allow a train to pass. This gave the two of them a moment to embrace.

At that very moment, Mark noticed a vehicle pull up alongside theirs. It appeared to be the same green military vehicle with the number forty-five in big bold white letters displayed on the trunk that he saw parked at the airport. It pulled up alongside Meghan and the two men inside, obviously military men from the looks of their uniforms, scrutinized them as if they were criminals on the Bureau of Space Investigation's most wanted list. Mark peered into the vehicle and realized that the driver and passenger looked familiar.

"I've seen these guys somewhere before, somewhere during my mission," he avowed.

"Maybe it's just routine for these guys to follow anyone who's been exposed to government classified information; you know the kind I came across during my mission," he substantiated.

They tried to keep a straight face, but the agents watched them very closely. This made Mark a little nervous.

"Seems like someone is interested in us," he said profoundly.

Meghan finally turned and noticed the agents staring at her. She decided to give them the look over as well. She noticed that the one closest to her had short dark hair, a scroungy moustache and a ruddy complexion that extended from his nose to the vertex of both cheeks. He also had acne, which was quite noticeable. She thought he looked absurd but spared herself from laughing disrespectfully in his face. She swallowed her laughter with a simple smile and nod. The agent tightened the knot on his black tie and pushed it up against the collar of his crisp white shirt. He straightened the collar and reciprocated with a smile which appeared to be more of a grin. Confused, Meghan quickly turned back towards the road and as the last car of the freight train finally passed with a gust of wind, the barrier arms lifted. At that moment, the green military vehicle with the number forty-five displayed on its trunk in white letters quickly sped off ahead of them.

It didn't take long to arrive home and as they pulled into the driveway, Mark couldn't help but notice how quaint and lovely everything looked.

The grass was trimmed, the flower beds were neat and well-kept, and everything was exactly how he left it many years ago.

"I see you've kept the place up quite well. I'm impressed."

"Don't thank me. Thank the landscapers," Meghan said proudly.

"Landscapers? You hired landscapers?"

Meghan laughed.

"No, I'm just kidding. Harry takes care of it and does a really nice job I must say."

Mark paused to think. The name sounded familiar. Then he remembered.

"Harry? You mean my old friend Harry Woods? Have you two been keeping in touch? By the way, where is he? Is he still here in town?"

"Oh yes, Harry still lives here in town. He's involved in sports and coaches the little league soccer games. Right now, he's either playing soccer or at his girlfriend Nina's house." Meghan broke off from the conversation.

"I have a surprise for you," she delightfully interjected. She took Mark by the hand and brought him around to the back of the house. As they turned toward the bend in the walkway Mark was welcomed by loud barking. He looked in the direction where it was coming from and saw Rex for the first time.

"Who is this majestic creature?" he said as he cautiously walked towards the dog.

"Honey, you stay right here."

Meghan went towards Rex and gave him a command. He immediately stopped barking and came up to meet Mark.

"Honey, this is Rex."

Rex playfully sat on his hind legs and lifted his right front paw to Mark as if to say hello in his own special language. Mark shook his paw and hugged Rex.

"Thank you for protecting my future wife."

He then turned to Meghan and exclaimed, "Honey, this is amazing. I'll have to reward Rex for a job well done."

This brought a glow to the dog's eyes, as he lifted his left ear indicating curiosity, but then relaxed them naturally showing that he was happy Mark was home.

CHAPTER 5

LOOKING BACK

Meghan woke at dawn to the soft susurration of the leaves that had been her cradlesong through the night into the early morning, becoming a fervent rustling, loud enough to drown out the choristers of birds outside gorging on seeds. Suddenly, a red-tailed hawk circling above descended out of the sky from behind a tall spruce tree and disseminated them. They flew in all directions hoping to evade the danger, which ended in an unsuspected jay getting caught in the hawk's clutches and carried off. Luckily Meghan didn't witness this and would have felt terrible if she did. As she turned over, she noticed that Mark was not lying beside her. She immediately jumped up and began calling out his name. Not hearing a response, she began searching for him. She looked all throughout the house and saw no signs of him. She became puzzled. She went into the kitchen and heard noises coming from the backyard. It sounded as if Mark had found himself a four-legged playmate. She opened the door to the backyard and called out to him.

"Good morning dear, shouldn't you be in here with me?"

Mark smiled and went over and gave her a huge kiss.

"Good morning sunshine. I didn't want to wake you and so I came out here to get acquainted with Rex."

"Okay, you guys can continue to get acquainted. Breakfast will be done soon so hurry up."

Meghan went back into the kitchen and started preparing breakfast. She reminisced back to the last time she prepared breakfast for Mark. This was many years ago. She remembered he was somewhat picky, yet always a hearty eater and liked seven eggs over easy with four beef sausages, six granary rolls with mayonnaise, cream cheese, and orange marmalade. She remembered he preferred orange over apple juice, a tall glass of milk and always had to have at least one full cup of black coffee with a shot of whiskey. He always said that whiskey stimulated his imagination.

After preparing the breakfast table, she went over to the window and called out to him.

"Mark, breakfast is ready."

"I'll be right in," he replied as he threw one last ball out into the garden as Rex went chasing after it. This gave Mark an opportunity to join Meghan for breakfast. Once inside he headed straight towards the laboratory to wash his hands before sitting at the oak dining table. He took a sip of spiked coffee and then picked up a copy of the morning edition of the *newspaper*. He scrutinized the front cover, turned a few pages, took another sip of coffee, and then placed the newspaper down on a small end table.

"I'm so jealous," Meghan joked coquettishly.

"What do you mean?" he asked as he spread some mayonnaise on a toasted granary roll, trying hard not to crumble it in the process.

"Well, I was looking for us to share a little-grown folks time this morning, but Rex took that away," she confessed before sipping on a cup of Earl Grey tea, which she always blended with honey, ginger, and lemon bits.

Mark laughed and admitted, "Sweetheart, there's going to be more than enough playtime for us."

He reached over the table and gently placed her hand in his.

"I love you," he proposed looking her straight in her beautiful blue eyes.

"And I love you too, so now finish your breakfast so that we can get this day started. We must go see Harry later so that you can catch up with the news."

*　*　*　*　*

The afternoon began to bring partly cloudy skies. It appeared there might be rain later, but Mark wasn't worried the least. It would soon be time to meet with Harry at the games and he wanted to catch up with his dear old friend. While he was getting dressed, he thought about his friendship with Harry over the years. His thoughts took him back to the time when they were street racers in their youth, as well as the many girlfriends they both dated. He thought about their devilish attributes that were superseded by attending church every Sunday. He thought about their dreams of the future where Harry always said he wanted to have a wife, kids, lots of money, and live in a big palace. He wondered if any of that ever happened to him.

*　*　*　*　*

It was a short drive to Quaker Field where the soccer game had already started. The crowds sitting in the wooden bleachers were cheering from both sides.

Meghan and Mark pulled up to the parking lot located on a landing overlooking the soccer field. There were steps leading down from the parking area which made it convenient to access the field.

Meghan leaned against her car smiling as Mark descended the steps from the side. As he walked towards the field, Meghan noticed him suddenly holding his stomach as if to be in pain.

"Honey are you okay?" she shouted.

He turned and noticed her expression and immediately took a deep breath, straightened up and replied, "I must be hungry; stomach's growling."

This assured Meghan that things were not as serious as she thought, and she smiled.

"I love you," she said as she tossed her flaxen hair.

He continued walking towards the field and Meghan wasn't sure whether he heard her or not.

As he entered the field Harry turned and glimpsed him from the side but did not know who he was. It had been years since they last saw one another, and it was evident that Mark's appearance changed. Just the same, Mark noticed that Harry looked totally different but still had retained his prominent characteristics.

Harry then turned to one of the players on the yellow team who just intercepted a field goal from the opposing green team. He shouted, "Pass it, yeah, whoa!"

Mark walked over to Harry a little hesitantly but with excitement.

"Which one of those bad boys is yours?"

Harry didn't turn around to see who was talking but responded anyway.

"They're all my boys," he pointed out proudly.

"I knew that," Mark responded energetically.

At that moment Harry recognized the voice as someone from his past and turned to see who it was.

"No way, Mark, is that you?" he asked ecstatically.

He then turned to his assistant coach, who was clearly a robot, and motioned for him to take over coaching the game.

Harry and Mark hugged each other and laughed as Meghan watched every moment. She then smiled and slowly walked towards them.

"Man, you look great. When did you get back in town? Shouldn't you be home with Meghan?"

At that very moment, Meghan walked up and grabbed Mark by the hand.

"Hello Harry, I thought you'd be pleased to see him."

"I am; he's my buddy and we haven't seen each other in years."

"I see you have a lot going on for you," Mark said inquisitively.

"Yeah, yeah, everything is good; I have a beautiful fiancé; what more can I ask for."

He then turned his attention back to the game as a member of the yellow team scored a point bringing the score 2_nil.

The crowd roared with excitement.

"A star; look at him go," Mark said referring to the youngster who just scored.

"I am so proud of you man," he exclaimed.

"That's what friends are for, besides we go way back."

"Hey, I want to thank you for taking care of Meghan while I was gone; you are truly a good friend."

"Don't mention it."

* * * * *

It was evening. Mark lay in bed listening to the rain beat against the windowpane. He wondered when it would stop. Meghan was in the den going over her plans for this evening. He called out to her.

"Honey, did you know the forecast called for rain this evening?"

Meghan was a little nervous because of the plans she made for Mark's welcome home party tonight at the bar and grill. She went into the bedroom and sat on the edge of the bed.

"No, I didn't but I wanted us to go over to the bar and grill to have dinner and cocktails."

"When are we leaving sweetheart, I'm starving?" Mark asked impatiently.

"I know that. I noticed you holding your stomach earlier today on the field and you looked hungry."

Mark reflected on what happened earlier as he went onto the field. He searched within himself to try and figure out what occurred, but to be honest - he never experienced the feeling he had today, and as far as he could tell, it was only hunger pains.

"Yes honey, I'm fine. What time are we going to have dinner?"

"I think you should get up and take a shower and start getting dressed right now," she hinted as she planted a kiss on his lips and went back into the den.

Mark gradually rose out of bed, stretched his muscles and walked into the den to find Meghan standing next to the window looking onto the garden. He walked over to her.

"I missed you so much and I'm going to prove it later tonight," he said.

He took her in his arms and they passionately kissed as if they wanted to forget anything and everything they had on their agenda for the evening. But Meghan knew she had made special plans for his welcome home party and that she had to be there to coordinate it all.

"Honey take your shower. I've already laid out your clothing for this evening."

Mark slowly walked towards the bathroom then shouted back, "Do I have any white shirts?"

It was only a short distance from the house to the grill. There was still a light drizzle of rain, but not enough to stop Mark's friends from coming out to welcome him back into society. As they pulled up to the restaurant in their stylish vehicle, the valet attendant opened the doors and Mark and Megan stepped out looking quite posh. The valet took the vehicle and parked it as they walked hand in hand towards the door of the grill. The maitre'd greeted them with a smile, opened the door, and looked at Mark and said in a heavy French accent *"Good evening sir, welcome home."*

As the door opened the music inside was festive while a group of familiar faces shouted "'Surprise! Surprise! Welcome home!"

Right away Mark noticed people that he had not seen in years. His friends Brian, Harry, Nina, his brother Domonic and his girlfriend Ashley were all there. Mark could not believe that he was back home with all his longtime friends, people that knew him from when he was a youth.

"I knew you would be surprised," Meghan said as she ran her hands through her hair.

Mark was so overjoyed that he turned to his friends and expressed his feelings.

"Thank you. This is unbelievable. It feels so good being home especially amongst all of you. You have me feeling exceptionally good right now. I mean, I really appreciate this. You can't understand how I feel. I'm just so glad to be back here with all of you," he confessed with a smile.

He continued to speak with his guest when without warning he felt a sharp pain in his stomach, which caused him to grimace and hold his abdomen. Meghan noticed the change in his disposition and rushed to his side.

"Honey, are you okay? You're holding your stomach just like earlier today."

But just as quickly as it happened, the pain was gone, and Mark stood erect as if nothing ever occurred.

"I'm good, just a little hungry."

At that moment Brian walked over to Mark to shake his hand.

"I'm glad you're back," he said excitingly. He gave Mark a pat on the back, another handshake and they both hugged one another.

Domonic observed his brother and Meghan from a distance before walking over to speak.

"Have a seat you two, relax, and enjoy the rest of the evening."

"Wait for a second, let me say thank you to my guests," Mark asked.

"I appreciated all of your good wishes while I was away, I love you all."

This stirred up applause from the guests in attendance that then joined in unison singing *'for he's a jolly good fellow…that nobody can deny'*.

Meghan was feeling good about the gathering and decided to excuse herself to go to the laboratory. While there she looked in the mirror to fix her hair and makeup and realized that she didn't have her necklace.

"Well, wouldn't you know it," she confessed.

"I need to get my necklace out of the car."

She went over to Mark and excused herself. She then went out to the car, opened the door on the passenger side and looked inside for her necklace.

"Now where did I put this?" she said as she searched the various compartments.

She touched the fingerprint recognition on the glove compartment, it opened and there underneath a handkerchief was the necklace; an Egyptian ankh pendant hanging from a gold chain that Mark had given

her ten years ago. He said it came from an undisclosed Egyptian tomb in the Valley of the Kings and had special powers. It was given to him by a colleague in Afghanistan and he gave it to her as a token of his love.

She looked in the mirror of the visor and put the necklace on.

"Better!" she said as she fiddled with the pendant.

"Now back to the party before I'm missed."

While returning, Meghan noticed a strange vehicle right outside of the venue and the person inside looked familiar. The car itself was a futuristic vehicle, the likes of which Meghan had not ever seen before. What was remarkable about this vehicle was that it had the features to both fly and drive based on zone. Meghan knew right then and there that the owner of that vehicle must be someone of authority. As she stared profoundly at the person inside the vehicle, she experienced a series of flashbacks as she tried to figure it all out. *I've seen that face before* she thought. *It appeared to be the same person who pulled up next to Mark and me at the train stop as we drove from the airport.*

This puzzled Meghan and prompted her to go over to the vehicle and ask questions. As she approached it, she waved to the driver to get his attention. He slowly let down the window.

"May I help you?" he asked in a foreign accent.

"Oh, I'm sorry. You look familiar. I thought you were someone I knew," she nervously replied.

It was then that Meghan confirmed that it was the same universal intelligence officer that pulled up next to her when she was driving Mark home that day. She noticed his scroungy moustache and ruddy cheeks, the slight rosacea, but only this time he was dressed in casual attire instead of the military uniform he wore that day.

"Are you here to celebrate with us?"

"Well, I guess I am part of the celebration," he replied.

"Do you mind if I ask you your name?" Meghan asked nervously.

"My friends call me Ricardo."

"So, are you here to celebrate with us?"

"No, I'm just here waiting for someone."

Meghan then gave him a look of discernment. It was obvious that the guy's reason for being there was trumped up and there appeared to be some unforeseen force behind his reasoning. Whether it was negative or positive - Meghan didn't have time to think about it right then and walked back towards the venue. Ricardo pulled out a video camera with a built-in bionic ear listening device.

"I can't let anything stop me from getting what I came here for," he said aloud while videotaping all the action inside through the large glass windows of the diner. He was able to capture Mark socializing with all the guests. So sharp were the visuals that he was even able to read their lips as they conversed.

"I got all of you" he bellowed to himself as he videotaped the action inside.

*　*　*　*　*

Everybody appeared to be having a good time at the party, all seated around Mark, conversing, and asking questions.

"So, tell us about your mission?" Brian asked inquisitively.

Mark looked at his guests with a somewhat bitter-sweet smile and moved his head in an almost imperceptible nod as if to say, "no way."

"Now you guys know I can't talk about that. What happens in operations stays in operations."

Outside of the bar and grill, Ricardo had just completed his videotaping and wrapped up his recording of the invited guests at the party.

This is all the evidence I need he thought to himself as he placed his camera into the carrying case. He then put the case on the front passenger seat of his vehicle before starting it up and driving off. It seemed he drove at least one hour north of the bar and grill before making a left turn onto an isolated dirt road. He then drove the length of it. The road was marked with signs that read *No Trespassing*. After driving another 30 minutes he finally reached a huge gate with a sign that read *Private Property - Keep Out!* As he approached the gate, he pulled up outside of it and was immediately recognized by a burly Russian security guard whom he spoke to in fluent Russian. The guard then issued his security clearance.

He then drove a few kilometres through the gate up to a four-story building and parked outside of it. There were only a few other vehicles parked alongside it and one was the black Hummer that was driven by his brother Nate.

Ricardo got out of his car, grabbed his camera bag with the recordings and proceeded to the outside lift. He typed in a code on the keypad on the wall and immediately the door opened. Once inside he flashed a badge, which allowed access to the underground laboratory floor units. He then pressed the button that read 'B2' and the lift began to descend to the sub-levels. After a few seconds the door opened, and Ricardo meticulously walked towards Laboratory A.

As he reached the door, he pressed a call button which sent a message inside indicating that he was out front. For security purposes, a dome centred overhead camera captured a 360° image of him and transmitted it into the security verification system. Once the system recognized him, a 15.24 centimetres thick steel door opened allowing him to enter the laboratory.

The atmosphere inside the laboratory was eerie with gloomy cobwebbed lighting fixtures, which hung like chandeliers in an old Gothic castle. The faces of the overworked scientists, who focused on completing their experiments, looked like aliens from another planet.

The laboratory was the size of a spacecraft hanger and housed enormous electrical equipment and mechanical devices used for the maintenance of spacecraft. Off to one side, a few groundbreaking experimental researchers, who appeared to be speaking an alien language, recreated the forces of wind power - inside a gigantic tubular can.

"Hey Nate, how's it going? I have something for you," Ricardo said as he placed his camcorder on a table. Nate, who was pre-occupied with a laboratory task briefly stopped to listen to what Ricardo had to say.

"What do you have there? For your sake I hope it's something good or else I'm going to be angry with you for coming in here interrupting me in the middle of my experiment."

"Nate just look, and you'll see what brought me here. Would I come this far for nothing?"

Nate stopped his work and walked over to the table and lifted the camcorder. He looked at Ricardo briefly then pressed the silver play button. After about two minutes of viewing the video, Nate was shocked at what he saw.

"No, how could this be!" he shouted angrily. He then walked over to Ricardo and aggressively grabbed him by the shirt collar.

"Fix this right now or else."

"Alright brother," Ricardo replied brushing off Nate's hands.

"I understand the way you feel but don't you ever grab me like that again."

Ricardo brushed himself off and angrily headed towards the exit of the laboratory. He boarded the lift and headed up to the parking area. He jumped into his vehicle, started the engine, and furiously drove towards the gate.

"Is everything okay?" the security guard asked.

Ricardo looked at him, frowned his face and replied *"Naduvat!"*

The guard gave Ricardo a quizzical expression before giving the cue for the gate to open, and like a madman, Ricardo raced through. It was obvious he was on a mission that he must complete or else he'd have to suffer the wrath of Nate.

CHAPTER 6

BLOWN AWAY

As the party came to an end, it was obvious that everyone had a great time. But things were only getting started. Mark and Meghan decided to carry the party over to their beautiful home and those who were ambitious enough went along for the ride. Not only did they stay the night, continuing where they left off at the diner, but the next day they woke early to a delicious breakfast prepared and served by a staff of robot chefs and waiters. They later amused themselves by playing backgammon, chess, card games or sunning themselves on the patio by the swimming pool as a robot band played futuristic music. Still, others indulged in intellectual conversation and watched vintage movies in a small cinema that Mark had built into the basement of his house. Not many people knew he was an avid collector of Ian Fleming movies and there could never have been a better time than now to show off his extensive collection.

Harry and Nina loved Fleming's James Bond films and took time out to relax on the blue leather directors' chairs with oversized pillows to view some of the films. Harry was curious why Mark was such an Ian Fleming aficionado and posed a few questions. This is something he never knew about his best friend.

"Tell me, what holds your interest in the character of James Bond?"

"Well, Harry, for the record, Ian Fleming was an Englishman who was an author, journalist, and naval intelligence officer who was best known for his spy novels."

"Then is that what sparked an interest in him, the intrigue, the espionage, the spy versus spy drama?"

Mark laughed and then replied.

"No, but one thing that sparked my interest was in finding out his father was a Member of Parliament for Henley."

"Weren't you born in Henley?"

"No, but as you might very well know, I studied at Henley for several years before coming here to the states and know it quite well. It was like a shot in the dark, but I survived it. I like the fact that while working for Britain's Naval Intelligence Division during the Second World War, Fleming was involved in espionage as well as planning and overseeing two intelligence units. His wartime service and his career as a journalist provided much of the background, detail, and depth of the James Bond novels."

"That's quite interesting, I never knew this and only thought the guy was a writer," Harry replied.

"What was your favourite Bond movie might I ask?"

"Casino Royale," Harry answered.

"Interesting, did you know it was Fleming's first book?"

"I didn't know that."

"Did you know that Fleming also wrote science fiction?"

"I didn't know that either even though I detected a bit of science fiction fantasy in his stories."

Mark left Harry and Nina watching the conclusion of *Casino Royale*, while he made his way back upstairs to check on the others. He looked at his watch and saw that it was approaching eleven o'clock. As he entered the main living room, it appeared that everyone stopped what they were doing to give him their undivided attention.

"Guys, I have something I'd like to share with you since you're all sober from last night's festivities."

Everyone laughed and focused on Mark, though Brian appeared restless and thought this would be a good time to be sarcastic.

"Let me guess; another one of those fantastic stories from your poignant childhood I presume."

This gave rise to a small uproar of laughter. But among those, Mark was the least bit jovial and looked at Brian shaking his head showing his contempt for his cynical remark. It was obvious that he was not amused by Brian's statement and he tried his best not to show his dismay. Instead, he gave a fake laugh which turned out to be more of a grin than anything else. Though they were friends, Brian had a bit of disdain for Mark, while Mark wanted nothing more but to be a good leader.

After watching the movie, Harry and Nina came up the stairs from the basement and joined in with the others who were discussing plans and strategies.

"Hi, did we miss anything?" Harry asked.

"You're just in time. You guys can have a seat."

"No, seriously, listen. I know you've been waiting on things to get back to how they were before, and I want to show you what I promised

I would, but first, let's get these vehicles back into the race," Mark conceded.

It appeared that several of his colleagues were puzzled by his comment and started talking amongst themselves. They didn't quite understand his logic and didn't know what to think. This comment especially seemed to agitate Domonic and he spoke out in contempt. This was somewhat peculiar as most have always seen him treat his brother with deference, at times even admiration, but he never went this far to oust him, especially at such a sensitive time in front of his dear friends.

"No, not this time; you can count me out. You know what happened the last time. I will not allow myself to be a part of this mechanical morass; it just doesn't fit into my equation" he rebuked appearing to be very angry over something in the past that was still haunting him.

He rose from the sofa and angrily walked towards the front door. He paused briefly and turned back toward Mark and his guests.

"I knew you were going backwards with this. You can count me out. I'm stepping outside to get some air."

Mark felt his disappointment and tried to compromise with him.

"Well, why not listen first to what I have to say at least for a moment."

"No way," Domonic said disappointedly as he turned and looked at Mark, shaking his head.

"Not this time brother."

He then proceeded towards the door. As he opened the door Ashley stood up, asked to be excused and ran out after him.

"Domonic, stop acting as if someone owes you," she said to him as he walked through the garden towards his car parked out on the curb.

"At least listen to what Mark has to say."

"No, I'm not going there with him."

Ashley was shocked at Dominic's attitude. She thought he had a chip on his shoulder because he now must play the little brother again. He had become used to being in control when Mark was away on his mission.

"Just stop, why don't you hear what he has to say?"

"Because I'm not interested, listen, I've already been through this and I don't want to go through it again. I have my reasons. You should respect that."

"Domonic, if you walk away without even trying to understand, you might regret this."

Domonic stopped a little and pondered Ashley's last statement but then he continued to get into his car and without looking back he drove off leaving everyone puzzled.

Ashley looked up into the sky as if she was expecting some great explanation to appear written in the clouds. Her eyes were pregnant with tears, but she forced herself to hold them in. She then turned and walked back across the lawn towards the front door. Rex ran up to her expecting a pat, but Ashley didn't acknowledge him. He lowered his head and disappeared towards the back of the house.

As Ashley entered the front door, all eyes turned in her direction.

"He just wouldn't listen to me," she said remorsefully, obviously feeling sorry as if it was her fault that Domonic disagreed with Mark's plan.

However, she then walked across the room and sat on a sofa next to Meghan and began to cry. Meghan reached out and compassionately placed her arm on Ashley's shoulders and gently handed her a soft napkin to wipe her tearing eyes. Ashley, finding comfort in being amongst friends, rested her head on Meghan's shoulder and continued to sob.

"Don't let it bother you, Ashley," Meghan said feeling a bit of regret for her friend.

"Domonic has never been able to see eye to eye with Mark and will never change. You know that, we all know that, and Mark knows it just as well. He hasn't changed."

Mark looked around at the remaining colleagues in the room and gathered enough courage to continue his speech. Before doing so, he looked again at his watch and noticed that it was approaching 11:57 AM.

"Alright, I guess I better hurry," he said discerningly as he continued his conversation.

"Now, I know you guys don't have a clue as to what NOV14135 is."

"What?" Harry responded surprisingly as he lifted his eyes from a science technology magazine that he'd been browsing through.

Suddenly, without warning, a loud explosion rocked the house. Everyone screamed in terror as the explosion ripped apart the basement and upper levels, breaking windows, smashing furniture, and sending everyone inside flying and crashing to the floor. But just as quickly as it occurred, it was over, though the destruction was devastating. The house, which stood proudly among others on the once manicured street, was now totally eradicated and several people were badly injured.

Brian was among those who were injured. Impulse compelled him to get up, but he involuntarily fell back to the floor like a wounded soldier. The impact was overwhelming and made him weak. The probability of internal injury or bleeding was severe. Mark was knocked to the ground but was still conscious. He was in pain but was able to get up just in time to see a green vehicle hastily leaving the area.

The pressure of the explosion had knocked Meghan to the floor. She had suffered injuries to her left groin and blood was running down the sides of her face from the impact of shrapnel and flying debris.

"My beautiful house is gone. What happened?"

Meghan couldn't believe that her once manicured home was now partially destroyed.

Mark quickly ran over to comfort her. He tried to lift her up but the pain in her back was too excruciating.

"Honey, are you okay?"

Meghan started to cry as Mark put his arms around her to supply comfort and support. Blood was running down her face and she was covered with debris from the shredded foundation.

"Where's Rex? Rex? Rex?" she cried out but there was no barking or any sound coming from the dog.

"Everything is going to be all right my sweet," Mark said as he kissed her and brushed off the dirt and grime from the bloody blast. All the while he's thinking who could have done this. He was still purporting Domonic's inexcusable exit from his home moments beforehand. He couldn't understand how his brother's supposedly feeling of affection turned into a feeling of bitter remorse and anger. What was he thinking and had he discovered something that would destroy us instead of wanting to revive a dream that belonged to us? He then called out to Harry.

"Get everyone out of the house. I'll be back."

Mark spots the keys to Meghan's vehicle on the floor, quickly grabs them and rushes out of the house. He jumps into the vehicle and speeds off in pursuit of the bomber.

Inside the house, Brian is attempting to get everyone out, but pain restricts his movement.

"Where is Nina? Has anyone seen Nina?" Harry shouts across the rubbles.

He looks around, but his vision is obscured by the vapours from busted pipes and concrete dust from the crumbled foundation of the den.

As he looks around he spots Nina, unconscious underneath the rubble. At the same time, Ashley also sees her and rushes to her aid.

"Oh no, Nina, come on now honey, wake up," he cried in anger.

Nina didn't budge and just laid there unconscious. Ashley noticed that she has a huge red scar with blood running out of her head. She must have suffered a blow which knocked her unconscious. Ashley became alarmed.

"We have to get her to the hospital right away. Help! Somebody, please help."

Her screams of terror alarmed Harry who quickly ran over to aid her.

"Is she okay?" he asked.

"She'll live," Ashley replied.

"But we still must get her to a doctor; there may be some internal injuries that need attention. Let's go."

CHAPTER 7

EMERGENCY

The smoke from the debris formed a small mushroom cloud in the sky above the house. Mark was able to see this in his rear-view digital display interface as he sped down the road in pursuit of an anonymous bomber. In his mind, Mark was determined to catch the suspect. The adrenaline in his body was in overdrive and this turned his personality completely around from good guy to bad guy.

Throughout all of this, Mark was thinking how important it was for him to get in touch with his brother because of his determination to get a message to him concerning NOV14135, the purple chemical substance he discovered while on his mission in Nanga Parbat.

He pressed the call button on the vehicles steering wheel which enabled it to react to voice recognition.

"Call Domonic," he commands. The vehicle responded with several tones before Domonic's automated message unit picked up. *'Please leave a message after the beep.'*

"Hey, give me a call now and meet me at the house; something has gone terribly wrong."

He clicks out of device mode and then continues his pursuit of the bomber. Suddenly, Marks mutation sets in and he almost loses control of the vehicle but just in time, his auto-control takes command. It is only after driving for ten minutes that he realizes that his pursuit is to no avail. He couldn't understand what might have transpired and allowed the culprit to escape. What if Domonic had something to do with this? Mark was totally perplexed.

He slowed down his vehicle and made a drifted U-turn and headed back home. From a distance, he could hear the humming of fire helicopters mixed in with the wailing of ambulances and drones flying overhead. The drones appeared to be heading away from the house and going in a different direction. This seemed to perplex Mark and so he stepped on the acceleration pedal and upped his speed.

As he approached the house, he noticed firemen spraying a blanket of foam from the helicopters above and from accessory fire vehicles on the ground. He also noticed a security barrier around the house with red and yellow hazard tape clearly stating the words *Crime Scene* and several police officers standing guard. He also noticed several bomb squad robots surveying the landscape surrounding the house looking for particles that might provide a clue to what triggered the explosion. While he does notice an ambulance and ER paramedics working on a patient, he doesn't realize that the patient is his best friend Harry, who suffered major injuries because of the explosion.

As he pulled up to the front of the house, he exited the vehicle and walked the grounds but was quickly stopped by an officer.

"Do not continue to move in my direction, you cannot proceed, this is a restricted crime scene area."

"Officer, what do you mean this is a restricted area? My name is Mark Parker, and this is my house. I live here," he said contemptuously and continued to walk in the direction of the house.

The officer put his hands on his neuro-disruptor and said, "Halt, stop it right there. If you continue to move forward, I'll fire upon you and desensitize the motor neurons of your body.

You do not have security clearance and you are not identified in my radar"

Mark found the actions of the officer to be somewhat peculiar and upon closer inspection, he noticed that he expressed no human emotions. Immediately, Mark realized that he was being confronted by a robot. Right away he figured that artificial intelligence deals with attempts to model and apply the intelligence of the human mind.

This made Mark reflect on his knowledge of robotics from studying computer science in the military. According to Isaac Asimov's three laws of robotics, a robot may not injure a human being or, through inaction allow a human being to be harmed.

Thus, a robot must obey orders given it by a human being. This made Mark think that this robot has already received orders from another human being to stop anyone who tries to cross its path. But can it be programmed to retract orders from the primary human source by a secondary human source? Thirdly, a robot must protect its own existence, which means that this robot feels that Mark's home is its existence. But then again, how does the human feel in this case?

The conclusion Mark came to is that eventually robots will control the world if we allow them to but the matter at hand was urgent and Mark knew that he had to try and come to some grips with this robot.

At that moment Brian, hearing the confrontation between Mark and the robotic officer, quickly wraps up a conversation with an emergency medical services officer and walks from behind the ambulance just at the nick of time.

"Mark!"

The robotic officer looked at Brian and asked him if he knew Mark.

"Yes, I know him. He is my friend and the owner of this house."

The robotic officer called his superior, a human detective dispatched to the crime scene, on his communications device. It was evident that this human contact was the primary controller of the robot officer and it was expected to follow his orders, but the robot officer's intelligence was given a test when Brian, who was already given security clearance, came over and stated that Mark owned the house. This immediately made the robot formulate a question from the order giver who the robot thought owned his existence.

He pulled the detective to one side and mechanically whispered something to him. Shortly thereafter the detective and the robotic officer walk back over to Mark. They immediately locked eyes with him as if to show their superiority.

"Hello, my name is Detective Wong. I'm with the Miami Police Department. Are you the owner of this house?"

"Yes, my name is Mark Parker. Can you tell me what is going on here?"

The detective looked around and then turned back to Mark.

"There is great danger here. It appears that someone wanted to kill you and as a result, they fire-bombed your house injuring some of the occupants. Where were you at the time the incident occurred?"

Mark angrily looked around and then held his head down in disgust, shaking it from left to right.

"I was there when it happened. I only left to try and pursue the culprit who might have set off the bomb. Look at these scars, my tattered clothes. Isn't that evidence enough that I was also a victim?"

The detective scrutinized Mark from head to toe paying close attention to a scar on his right forearm. He then continued with his questioning.

"Did you find him?" the detective asked.

Mark appeared to be isolated in his thoughts but after a brief hesitation, he answered the question.

"No, I did not."

Detective Wong whispered in the ear of the officer who then came over to Mark.

"We would like you to come down to police headquarters for routine questioning tomorrow morning at ten o'clock if you don't mind. We'd like to question you concerning this incident. We think it's our duty to help find out who'd want to bomb your home. Maybe your life is in danger but if so, then that means the lives of those close to you; your family, friends, and even loved ones might also be in danger as you can see by this incident which occurred," the officer said quite sternly.

Mark thought for a moment. He thought about Domonic, Meghan, his friends, the entire afternoon, this horrible incident that occurred. It didn't make any sense to him. Perhaps he might need the help of the UIO to figure this whole thing out and so he consented to meet them down at the police station the next morning at ten.

Mark was puzzled by this whole episode and didn't know what to do. He gazed up into the afternoon sky. It appeared gloomy, yet it was spring, seventy-five degrees – typically warm, overall just a beautiful evening. Even though the sun was setting, the magic hour aimed the remaining rays at him like giant floodlights in a theatre. So much was going through his head and he didn't know what to think, though his thoughts were mostly about Meghan and Domonic.

From a distance, Brian looked over at Mark and thought he might need someone to talk to. He walked over to him to try to break his concentration.

"Mark. Mark, hey Mark."

He didn't seem to hear Brian and so he called louder.

"Hey man, are you okay?"

"I've been calling out your name at least five times and you just looked up into the sky as if somebody up there was trying to communicate with you. Are you okay?"

"I'm alright. Where's Meghan?"

"Ashley has taken her and Nina to Metropolitan hospital."

Mark lowered his head in thought and then raised his head and called for Rex.

"Rex, Rex, where are you bud? Rex, Rex."

He looked around but there was no sign of his beloved Afghan. He then ran towards the back of the demolished house to see if he could find him.

"Rex, where are you buddy?"

There was no respond at all. He quickly walked back to the front of the house over towards Brian.

"The noise from the explosion might have frightened him and he must have run away. Dogs are pretty sensitive to danger, especially loud noises," Brian replied.

"What about Harry? Is he okay?"

"I was just speaking with the medic and he mentioned they're going to ride him over to the hospital and let the ER doctors take a look at him."

"Well Brian, can you go over with him and make sure he's okay?"

"Sure but watch those guys that you have to talk with tomorrow. They tend to be a little persuasive in their questioning, you know what I mean?"

"I hear you, Brian. Remember, I have a lot of military training in special operations and have been in high places with some high-ranking people. Those guys don't scare me."

Brian hesitated to answer but then had to remind Mark, "Well, you've also been in some pretty low places. Think about it."

Mark was abruptly taken back to reality and could do nothing about it. For a moment he dwelled in the unhappiness which had sunken deep within him. His emotions, stabilized by his constant battle with an invisible enemy, were obviously defined. He was now at a point in his life where it was all about moving forward with him. Nevertheless, he acknowledged his friend's statement.

"Thanks for reminding me Brian," he said before getting into his car and driving off. As he drove away, he couldn't help but think about what Brian mentioned to him. It was an unexpected reminder, but nonetheless, it was a reminder.

*   *   *   *   *

Later that evening Domonic showed up at a street racing event, 72 kilometres away from the house. It was in the downtown section of the city and so there were lots of people standing around. The tall buildings stood magnificently erect while the crowd cheered on the street racers as they lined up their vehicles. In the sky, vehicles flew overhead as this was a fly and drive zone.

All the while, Domonic appeared to be in deep thought.

"What am I doing here?" he asked himself. He started to reflect on the argument that occurred earlier at his brother's house. After spending some time thinking about the confrontation, Domonic decided to walk away and didn't realize he was being observed by Ryan, one of Nate's henchmen sitting not far away in his vehicle viewing pictures of Mark and his entire crew. Ryan received a message to terminate any one of them upon contact. That included Domonic as well.

Unaware of what was about to take place, Domonic was approached by Ryan.

"Nice ride you have there."

"Thanks. It's not mine though," Domonic said in a somewhat humble voice.

"So, you're driving another man's ride. Are you in the race?" Ryan asks sarcastically.

"No, it's my brother's car; I just came out for a breath of fresh air and chanced upon this event."

At that point, the racers started their engines and the race was about to get underway.

"By the way, I'm Ryan. I can have you in the next race. What do you say?"

Domonic pondered his question and thought whether he wanted to go with it or not. He then thought about the reason which caused him to leave his brother's house in an uproar, as well as his brother's decision to try and pick back up on getting the cars back out to race. He thought about all of that before making his decision.

"I'm Domonic. Thanks for the offer, but I'm good."

Ryan quickly sensed Domonic's naïve personality and started grinning sinisterly.

As Ryan walked over to his car, Domonic accessed his and prepared to drive back to his brother's place. He didn't want the day to go by without bringing closure to that earlier incident and started to show signs of remorse

"Leaving so soon," Ryan asked as Domonic started up his vehicle.

Domonic thought the guy was strange and ignored Ryan. He then started on his way home. No more than thirty seconds later, he saw a car quickly speeding towards him from behind. It pulled up next to him and he noticed that Ryan was behind the wheel.
"Where do you think you're going?" he asks grinning sinisterly.

Domonic noticed a slight change in Ryan's character and quickly sped away from him. Ryan caught up with him, giving Domonic a sense of hyperarousal, who then steps on the pedal and races off at top speed desperately trying to get away from this madman.

As they race through the city in a synchronous pattern, side by side just centimetres away from one another, cutting corners as sharp as razors, Ryan swiftly slams Domonic's car into the side of an office building in downtown Miami. The impact makes the car roll over several times and eventually lands on its roof.

Domonic, feeling traumatized, tries to hold on to his consciousness but is breathing heavily. Ryan returns to the crash site and pulls up right alongside of Domonic's wrecked vehicle. The passenger door is open and Domonic is fully exposed. His once white dress shirt is tainted with blood, while his tan leisure cotton pants are ripped apart and all bloody. The only thing keeping him from falling from his vehicle is the fact that he is still strapped in by the seat belt.

"What is going on? I'm bleeding man, help me."

Ryan looks at him and grins. He then steps out of his car with his neuro-disruptor and quickly walks towards Domonic.

"Did someone say help? The only help you're going to need right now is this here," Ryan says branding his neuro-disruptor as if to intimidate Domonic.

All at once, Domonic starts to feel drained and dizzy. An odd gurgling sound was coming from him and laboured breathing altered his attempts to speak. He gasped for air and slowly started to recover.

"What's going on, what's this?"

Ryan looked at him and shook his head.

"You just got yourself into some big trouble kid," he says amid kicking Domonic in the head with his boot and knocking him out cold.

"On second thought you're coming with me," he says before firing one beam from his neuro ripping off Domonic's seat belt causing him to fall to the ground.

CHAPTER 8

THE INTERROGATION

The next morning, Mark awoke from his sleep still feeling confused about his brother's actions leading up to the explosion. It was as if he had a sixth sense and felt that Domonic might be in trouble. He thought to himself and concluded that he'll just have to continue to be puzzled until he speaks with Domonic; then maybe he'd be able to explain what's happening in his life.

In the meantime, it was approaching ten o'clock and Mark had to rush to make it to his appointment at the police station on time.

* * * * *

It didn't take long to arrive at the station. As he entered the building, he noticed a woman sitting and sobbing uncontrollably. He wondered if he should go over and offer his help but decided against it since he already had enough problems of his own to deal with.

Mark walked over to the front desk and was a bit intimidated by the desk sergeant, who sat high in a brown leather chair encapsulated with gold nail heads. The desk itself was made from grey marble and the sergeant, who gave a twitch at his moustache, wore a navy-blue authoritative uniform with a six-point gold shield over his left breast pocket, three evidently earned diagonal stripes on both shoulders and a name tag that read Sergeant McFarland. His gold horn-rimmed glasses sat at the tip of his nose and he looked down at Mark as if he were an ordinary common criminal. The illusion of being ordinary seemed to mesmerize Mark, but he quickly snapped out of this dream state back into reality. He had a job to do and he didn't like wasting his time on things of this nature.

He proceeded to speak scrupulously.

"Good morning. I was asked to come down for questioning by Detective Wong."

93

Sergeant McFarland continued to stare at Mark for a few seconds before commenting.

"May I see your government identification card?"

Mark carefully reached into his back pocket for his wallet - took out the card and gave it to the desk sergeant.

"Is this going to take long?" he asked going against the grain of always being commended for his virtue of patience.

"Long is such an inappropriate way of putting it, but yes, it's going to take a while. We were expecting you. Why don't you have a seat; in a moment Detective Wong and Detective Miller would like to question you regarding an explosion which occurred yesterday at 8160 North Hudson Street. Officer Baylor will escort you into the interrogation room shortly when they're ready."

Mark walked over to the wooden benches located against the walls of the precinct. As he sat and waited, he looked around at all the pictures of law enforcement officers who had succumbed in the line of duty. It was a distressing sight, one that he wasn't in the mood to fathom. He then thought again about his brother Domonic. He thought that his timing that day could not have been any better because he left the house right before the explosion; paradoxically his behaviour was somewhat suspect. It made him wonder whether Domonic had anything to do with the bombing because it was typical of humans to think out all the facts leading up to a criminal investigation before being questioned by law enforcement. And he wanted to make sure he had all his facts in order.

It wasn't long before he was approached by a police officer.

"I'm Officer Baylor. Can you come with me?"

"Where are we going?" Mark asked unpretentiously.

"No need to be alarmed. I'm taking you into a special room where two detectives are going to ask you questions concerning the incident."

Mark followed the officer. They walked a few meters past the desk sergeant, made a left turn down a hallway before walking a few more meters to a grey metal door, which looked as if it was made of steel from an old battleship.

Officer Baylor opened the door and they both went inside. There was a grey metal table about 2.1 meters by 7.0 meters, with three hard black chairs, one on the furthest end and two on the end nearest the door. There was also a one-way mirror where a surveillance operation could take place without the person knowing who was looking in on them; a somewhat obsolete form of surveillance now that 360° cameras were embedded inside and outside of the ceilings and roofs of buildings everywhere. There was also an ashtray and a pack of cigarettes; the pack had three Chinese characters on it; *Furongwang* was the name. They appeared to be expensive; thin in width; a royal blue filter with a golden crown on one side of it.

Officer Baylor pointed to the chair furthest away from the door, the one by itself.

"You can have a seat over there. You can also have a smoke if you'd like to. The detectives will be with you shortly." He then closed the door.

Mark went over to the table to observe the pack of cigarettes. He took one out and lit it, took a few puffs and quickly disposed of it. He was never a smoker and didn't want to start now.

Without warning, Mark's thoughts took him back to the days of working as a special operations officer on *Project 70*. He was very familiar with the sound and the environment he currently was in as part of his duty was interrogation and guarding prisoners at a military camp in Iraq. The sound of slamming doors with heavy iron gates where captured war prisoners were impounded was still embedded in his head. That sound never changes, and it never goes away; it stays with you.

During reminiscing, the door opened, and Detective Wong came in with a folder containing documents. Immediately following him was another person, dressed in a dark business suit, identical to the one Detective Wong adorned. Mark immediately stood up.

"Oh no, you don't have to stand. Please remain seated," Detective Wong insisted.

Mark resumed sitting. The detective then placed the folder on the table and he and his partner seated themselves in the two chairs closest to the door.

"I'd like to introduce you to Detective Miller. He will assist me in this case. By the way, Detective Miller is also a special unit bomb squad agent with the International Bureau of Space Investigation (IBSI). If you ever plan on leaving town or travelling into space during the time of our investigation, please understand that his bureau is also responsible for the issuance of space travel passports."

This didn't bother Mark the least and all he wanted to do was to get to the bottom of this whole thing and move on with his life. He had already spent ten years on a special military assignment, and he had already seen the interrogation of suspected terrorists repeatedly.

Detective Wong opened the folder and took out some documents.

"Mark, I'd like you to look over these documents and make sure you understand everything that is stated on them. Afterwards, I'd like you to sign them."

Mark looked at the documents and found them to be suitable for his signature.

"Now Mark, we're going to ask you some questions that you might not like but please, don't become offended or angry and just answer them to the best of your ability. Agree?"

"Agree," Mark replied.

Detective Miller reached over and took a cigarette from the box and lit it. He took one puff and inhaled quite deeply and blew out several smoke rings. Mark watched as the smoke rose above his head and seemed to widen as it reached the ceiling. It then descended and settled around him. This irritated Mark, and he kindly asked the detective to put out the cigarette.

"I'm sorry the smoke is bothering you and might interfere with you answering the questions correctly, so I'll kindly put it out."

He dropped the cigarette to the floor and stepped on it with his left shoe. Mark looked down and noticed that the detective was well polished and wore brown Gucci loafers. The detective than continued his questioning.

"Did you intentionally plan to kill your friends?" he asked imprudently.

With this first question, Mark looked up and became grossly angry and an outburst occurred.

"I'm very sorry, but I don't know what the heck you're talking about. I don't go around killing people. That was my family, my friends and not to mention, I was there when the explosion took place. Why would I want to kill anyone, let alone myself?"

The detectives looked at Mark and then turned to one another. Detective Miller shrugged his shoulder, cleared his throat from a slight congestion and lit another cigarette, blew a few smoke rings into the air before resuming the questioning.

"Have you ever associated yourself with terrorists or been involved with any terrorist groups or gangs?" he asked.

"No," Mark answered.

It was obvious that he was becoming annoyed by this form of questioning.

"You do know that this is an act of violence?"

Mark became puzzled by his comment and stared into the eyes of both agents.

"Who do you think I am?" he bellowed.

Detective Miller looked down and was puzzled by Mark's statement. He then turned to his partner and then back to Mark.

"It says here that you are a mechanical engineer and a previous street racer who once was in trouble? Correct? What do you know about this explosion tough guy?"

Detective Wong continued to look at his files and said, "You also participated in some sort of special operations for the government I see. We wouldn't want to blame you for something that you didn't do but if you cooperate with us, we can wrap this up rather quickly."

Mark looked down and started to think back about the interrogation procedures he executed when capturing suspected terrorists during his assignment. He thinks he made a few mistakes back then and doesn't want to have to go through this repeatedly.

Detective Miller then interceded and asked his partner to give him a copy of the vehicle files. He proceeded to flip through the papers until he came to a photo of a crashed vehicle. He then looked at Mark and questioned him.

"Do you recognize this vehicle?" he asked.

Mark looked surprisingly at the photo and replied vehemently, "Yes, that vehicle belongs to me. What happened to it?"

"Mr. Mark, do you know anyone by the name of Domonic? We found this vehicle overturned and the computer inside of it identified him as the last scanned driver. Do you know him?"

Angrily, Mark jumped up out of his chair with a burst of uncontrollable energy. Both detectives jumped up to restrain him.

"Control yourself," Detective Wong said as his partner reached for his Taser.

Mark calmed down just as quickly as he lost his temper and apologized for his behaviour.

"I'm sorry, Domonic is my brother. Where is he? Is he hurt?"

"We did find his name in the technology system of the vehicle and therefore, he becomes a suspect in this case."

"He had nothing to do with this. He's my brother. I gave him the authorization to drive the vehicle. Leave him out of this."

The detectives decided then that they were going to finish questioning their suspect later. As they excused themselves from the room, Mark felt irritated and stressed. He shook his head, dismayed at this whole episode, and just wanted to go home and forget about it. He wondered about his brother and wanted to find out if he was okay.

Minutes later both detectives came back into the room and sat down in their chairs. Despite Mark's earlier plea, Detective Miller lit up another cigarette, took a few puffs and then put it out.

"We unequivocally condemn any violence in this jurisdiction. Remember that. You can go home now but don't leave the region. We will call on you again soon."

CHAPTER 9

THE HIDDEN SECRET

Nimbostratus clouds covered the sky as rain fell heavy at times during the course of the evening. Mark and Meghan had just arrived for dinner at the bar and grill.

The ambiance was perfect. The diner wasn't crowded, perhaps the inclement weather had much to do with it, however, it was just right for Mark and Meghan. They made their way over to a candle lit dining table near the back corner underneath a colourful painting of a soccer player scoring a goal. There was quiet classical music playing on the public address system, the perfect musical accompaniment for a rainy evening. From this table, Mark had a perfect view of the entire dining area. Once seated the waiter brought over a bottle of Bordeaux, opened it and poured them both a glass.

As the music continued to play Mark looked Meghan in her eyes and smiled. She, in return, was impressed with him and she smiled back. It was obvious that she was the happiest person in the world.

"I cannot tell you how lucky I am to have such a beautiful partner as you," Mark said as he reached across the table and held her hands.

"And I can't tell you how safe I feel being with you," she replied.

"I pray that we never go through anything like what occurred the other day, ever again."

"I agree."

At that moment Brian entered the diner, folded his umbrella and handed it to the waiter at the door, who pointed him in the direction of the maitre'd. He walked over to the maitre'd who politely asked, "how can I help you?"

"I'm here to see Mr. Parker. He's expecting me."

"Right this way sir."

The maitre'd brought Brian over to the table right at the very moment when Mark and Meghan were expressing their affection for one another. He was able to overhear their conversation.

"Look you guys, I didn't come out on this rainy evening to hear a bunch of romantic talk. I'll never become a biomechanical engineer listening to this type of conversation. Can we change the subject?," Brian asked sarcastically.

Mark and Meghan both looked at him and laughed.

"What's going on Brian? Have a seat."

"Look, I hope you don't mind but I need to talk with you concerning new scientific evidence regarding the possibility of terraforming and colonizing Mars and..."

Mark instantly cut Brian off in the middle of his conversation.

"Brian, your timing is off by just a few hours."

He then turned towards a waiter who was several meters away and motioned to him to serve Brian.

The waiter immediately came over and poured him a glass of Bordeaux.

"Thank you for this glass of wine but..."

"Excuse me, hold your thought," Mark interrupted.

At that very moment, Mark's lapel pin telecommunications device started to vibrate indicating there was a call coming through. He glanced at his forearm device and noticed that it was Domonic calling.

"Please excuse me. I must take this call. It's my brother, I'll be right back."

Mark's device continued to vibrate as he stood up and walked over to a secluded area to answer the call.

"Hey, where are you? Are you okay?"

There was no reply.

"Hey, Domonic, are you okay?"

Still no one said a word.

There seemed to have been a long pause on the other end; a bit of silence and heavy breathing in the background.

Finally, a strange voice, unlike any he had ever heard, replied. It was somewhat mechanical and emotional, not quite a whisper yet clearly crisp and articulate.

"You listen and listen carefully. If you ever want to see your brother again, tell me now where you've hidden the substance?"

Mark listened to the sinister voice on the other end and was stunned by what he heard. He knew right away that this was not his brother's voice, yet he didn't have a clue as to whom it might have been. Nevertheless, he continued to ask questions.

"Who is this and what are you talking about? Where's my brother?" he asked the mechanical voice on the other end.

"I am someone from your past. I stumbled upon you near what appeared to be an ablated meteorite, but had I known it carried an alien substance that would have given me power over the universe; I would have destroyed you that very moment and taken the substance away with me. You were practically dead when I discovered you that night. Whatever the substance was, you were able to get to it before I did. It was only later while in my laboratory that I found traces of it on my clothing. It must have rubbed off on me when I tried to help you. I conducted an experiment, which proved the substance was an extreme source of energy, the likes never seen or discovered by man here on earth. It didn't take long to figure out that you were the only one who encountered it."

"And what is it you want from me?" Mark asked.

"Don't you worry just do as I say," the mysterious voice beckoned.

After a few seconds, Mark's forearm device voice recognition feature identified the caller as Nate Abboud.

"Nate, you coward. I should have known you were up to no good from the very start during our secret mission in Pakistan. What have you done to my brother?" Mark shouted uncontrollably while people in the restaurant began to curiously look back and stare at him. Brian quickly stood up from the table and walked over to Mark. He stopped and stared at him.

"What's going on? Is everything okay?" he whispered but Mark didn't respond; instead, he continued to listen to the voice on the call.

"There's a possibility that I am your worst nightmare and may have called to tell you that you'll never see your brother again," Nate taunted.

"If you touch one hair on his head I'll..."

Before he could finish his statement, he was interrupted by Nate.

"Let me guess – you're going to kill me? You idiot."

At that moment the device hung up. It left Mark puzzled and confused.

"Is everything okay Mark?" Brian demanded to know.

Mark shook his head as if to suggest that everything was okay, but in fact, it appeared to have only been a piece of that unsolved mystery, haunting him regarding the past.

As Mark and Brian approach Meghan back at the table, she quickly noticed the volatility of Mark's former personality had changed drastically. His lips were pursed, and his eyes were narrowed and red as he pulled his chair from the table and took a seat.

"Honey, I know you better than anybody else in this world and you look like you've just talked with a ghost."

Mark was still in shock and disbelief. His face had become pale and lacked expression, devoid of any warmth as if he were just a frame without a picture. His thoughts appeared to be frozen in time and his gaze was like a winter storm. Finally, he opened.

"It's Domonic, they've captured him," he said remorsefully.

Brian and Meghan looked at one another, with puzzled expressions, not comprehending any of this.

"Mark, what are you trying to say?" Meghan asked.

"Look, I know what you guys are thinking but it's time to let you know the truth."

"Time to let us know the truth. Get to the point mate. What are you trying to tell us?" Brian asked inquisitively.

Slowly, Mark gets up from his chair and meticulously begins to explain things. It was obvious he had something important to tell but he wanted to make sure it wouldn't go any further then the room.

"Look, I tried telling you guys earlier. Follow me and I'll explain; it's no longer safe here."

As they started walking towards the back of the diner, a familiar voice called out to them.

"Hey, where are you guys going?"

Everyone turned just in time to see Harry and Ashley walking to catch up to them.

"You're both just in time; Hey Harry, it's good seeing you, How are you feeling? "

"I'm as good as new, you know me."

"Ashley, great seeing you too. And by the way, how is Nina?"

Harry replied, "She's resting over at Metropolitan. The doctors said she'll soon be able to come home."

"That's good news," Mark replied as they continued to walk further into the rear of the diner.

Mark led the group to a bookcase, which moved to reveal a narrow passage. They walked a few kilometres through the moldy, concrete passage before entering a hidden chamber with folding gates. Mark then turned towards Meghan and walked over to her. He reached for her necklace, but she lightly backed away giving him a surprised look.

"What's going on?" she asked suspiciously.

"I am very sorry dear but I'm going to need this," he replied.

He then reached behind her neck as if hugging her and took off the necklace.

"But honey, you gave this to me to symbolize our eternal love and now you're taking it back?"

"Don't worry sweetheart," he said assuredly.

"I'll have something better for you in no time."

He kissed her and walked towards the wall. It was obvious Meghan was upset but she decided to hide her anger.

He then inserted the ankh into a keyhole then placed the palm of his left hand on the wall in a sequence pattern with the key to open the folding gates, revealing a secret door and an obsolete patterned lift. It looked as if it led to some secret experimental area.

"Wow! Is this a laboratory or what?" Ashley inquired.

"I wouldn't worry about it if I were you. Just follow," Mark replied.

"Where is this taking us?"

"Just relax, trust me; in time you will understand it all."

At that moment they continued to enter the lift which took them to an underground area. As the door opened, everyone stepped out and proceeded to walk through the corridor, past an old boiler room, leading to the main entrance of the laboratory. At that point, the door opened, and an automated system turned on the lights while a computerized female voice projected over a hidden PA system.

'Hello, my name is Kylie. Welcome.'

They continued to walk a few meters when Mark stopped, turned around, and delivered a message.

"What you are about to see must never be disclosed to anyone."

Just as quickly as he stopped speaking, he turned and continued walking towards another secret door. At the edge of the door was a locked box situated on the wall. Mark took his right index finger and placed it on the scan detector area of the box to unlock it. Inside there was a Kalimba, an ancient African musical instrument that he was taught to play when he was a child. His teacher, an old Nigerian griot named *Gbemisola*, was also a manservant to his father.

Mark picked up the small instrument and placed it in the palm of his left hand and plucked a strange melody on the metal tines attached to its small wooden board which produced tones. Suddenly, the secret door automatically opened slowly and they all anxiously waited to see what was behind it. A flash of iridescent light illuminated the foreground and an eerie gaseous hydrogen cloud rose from the room giving off a feeling of coolness. At that very moment, the door opened to reveal a room stored with vehicles in their transformed state. Everyone was stunned by the sight.

Not believing his eyes, Brian couldn't hold back his reaction.

"Is this some sort of joke?"

Mark looked at him and then turned and looked at everyone else.

"What you are all seeing is the basic transformed state of each machine."

Harry didn't know what to think and gave Mark the typical look of a confused person.

"What are you trying to tell us?" he asked.

"You mean to tell us these machines can change shapes and sizes?" Brian inquired.

"As you can see," Mark replied.

"This is amazing," Ashley added.

As they all continued to chat amongst themselves Mark called for their attention.

"Listen, it's much more than that; now, if you would allow me. This is what I've been trying to tell you before we became distracted back home; someone is after me, possibly all of us."

This comment really made everyone get off the edge and they all looked at one another as if they were about to call it quits.

"No way! Tell me something I don't already know," Brian said sarcastically.

Mark paused and looked around for a moment.

"His name is Nate Abboud, one of my old associates; we worked together in the past on a few government projects. He was later accused of espionage and that was the last I saw of him. During one of my missions, I came to discover a powerful energy source that I now hold, and he would do anything to get it from me and as you can see it has already started. If it ever gets into the wrong hands it may cause great harm to our world," Mark said gravely.

"So where is this source now?" Ashley asked.

Mark paused to think before answering the question. He looked around at the machines and then responded.

"No need to worry, it has been safely stored, some of it is inside each of these machines and myself."

Meghan became full of anger and disbelief at this whole conversation unfolding before her.

"So, I'm guessing now I should just relax and accept all that you have said and think that everything is okay?"

"What seems to be the problem?" Mark responded.

"What's my problem? You mean you kept all these secrets away from me for all these years and didn't tell me anything, not even gave me a clue that there was a dark side to you?"

"It wasn't the right time and besides, you knew that I was on a secret mission and never once did you ask questions. Why are you surprised now?" Mark asked.

The other people in the room didn't find this to be amusing nor appropriate yet they tried their best to ignore what was going on by scattering and inspecting the vehicles.

"Mark, that is not the way a relationship works; get me out of here. So wonder Domonic ran off the way he did. I don't blame him."

Upset, Meghan turned and walked towards an exit door. She had no idea where it linked to, but her anger prompted her to want to get away from Mark. Right now, she couldn't stand the sight of him and felt cheated. She felt he should have told her more about the dark side of his life.

Nevertheless, she was upset and didn't want to be bothered with anyone.

"Please don't do this to me now; I'm not perfect you know," Mark pleaded with her as she walked away.

Despite his pleas, Meghan left the room. Ashley found all of this to be appalling and shook her head.

"You know not everyone can handle a secret, especially after it's been exposed."

All while this was taking place, Brian was admiring one of the vehicles that caught his eyes.

"Now, where did a machine like this come from?"

Mark turned and looked around at the remaining individuals in the room.

"Guys listen. We have bigger problems ahead of us and all I want to know is who is with me and who isn't?"

Everyone paused and looked at one another.

"If we weren't with you I think we would have left when Meghan pulled out of here," Brian added jokingly.

"Hey smart mouth," Harry responded.

"Why don't you just speak for yourself?"

He then turned to Mark and said, "We've been friends forever; I'm in."

"Okay then, let's go find a way to get Domonic. Nate has him and wants the NOV14135, well, the novaerium. But first, let's get to the training ground."

"I have an idea. Why don't we just give him the substance," Ashley responded.

"Apparently you don't understand the power that novaerium possesses," Mark explained then continued.

"I can't even imagine what Nate would want to do with such power; remember it gives and takes life."

*   *   *   *   *

While Mark was preparing training gadgets, Brian continued to admire the many machines inside the laboratory.

"You know just looking at these awesome machines turns me on. You mind if I test drive one of them?" he asked.

Everyone looked at Brian and then focused on Mark, who released a sigh, shook his head at Brian and then walked over to the shelf to grab the forearm portable gadget controllers for the machines.

"Here, take one of these."

Mark handed everyone a flexible hologram and asked them to attach it to their forearm.

"Each one of these forearm hologram gadgets can control a machine from anywhere."

"Now that's what I'm talking about," Brian replied excitingly.

At that moment, Mark directed everyone to walk over to select a machine of their choice. Afterwards, he directed each of his crew to a cabinet, which held intravehicular pressure suits to be worn while operating the machines.

"These suits are adjustable and must be worn along with your seatbelts and headgear at all times while operating these machines."

Everyone looked amazed at their suits and gadgets.

"Make sure you remember to communicate using the wireless earpiece that is connected to your forearm device. I suggest you all turn it on now."

The team suited up, turned on their forearm communication devices, and selected a machine that was fully equipped with the highest standard of technology along with the chemical power of the novaerium. Each boarded their machines and closed the compartment.

"I always wanted to be a bubblehead," Brian said amusingly.

"Let's head out to the intergalactic space training ground to test our novaerium powered machines," Mark ordered.

At that moment, a secret door opened leading to an illuminated tunnel and the machines started to go through. It was a strange looking tunnel with odd dimensions and bright iridescent lights throughout as far as the eyes can see. They became brighter and more colourful as the convoy of machines made their way through as if it were an amusement park ride.

CHAPTER 10

THINK IT, IT DOES IT

The ride through the underground tunnel was brief and everyone made it safely. As they exited the tunnel, Mark led the team to the secret training ground. This was done by relaying a verbal message that was picked up by a microphone device on the computer inside of his machine, which was connected to everyone's micro wireless earpiece and forearm device. He encouraged everyone to use theirs in the process of communicating.

"Follow the programmed map on your display screens. We will all begin our training at that location but be mindful that there will be others there from out of space since this is an intergalactic space training ground," he relayed in a message.

"I'll race you," Brian said. At that moment they all broke format and raced off towards the location. Suddenly, Mark's machine disappeared into thin air.

"Mark? Where did you go?" Harry asked surprisingly.

No sooner than he expressed his thoughts Mark's car gave a monstrous roar and reappeared just ahead of his loyal companion.

"Wait one minute, did you guys see that?" Ashley asked.

"How did you do that?"

"Easy, just read the manual, and when you think it, it does it."

"Okay, let's see what mine can do," she asserted.

Ashley's machine transformed into a sleek miniature jet and took off towards the training grounds in a flash which left a burst of iridescent flames coming out of the multiple burners.

"Wow Ashley," Brian said astonished at what he just witnessed.

This amazed Harry as well.

"Think it, it does it, think it, it does it," Brian repeated to himself. Harry was known for not being able to control his thoughts and the fear of not knowing what to expect was evident in his voice.

"Okay, I'm going to think and..."

Before Harry could complete his sentence, his machine transformed into a phenomenal huge green and white robot that appeared to engulf him, taking over his body yet he was still able to control it, though the robot appeared to be out of control.

"Wow, can you believe this. Such versatility in mechanics," Harry exclaimed, amazed at his machines extraordinary ability to transform.

Suddenly, the robot fumbled while going through various astonishing manoeuvres. Harry tried to execute strategic moves inside the eye-catching robot but nevertheless, he enjoyed showing off the astounding versatility of his machine. This only led to him finally falling on his rear but quickly getting back up just in time to run and catch up with the rest of the team.

At that moment, in a show of ingenuity, Mark pulled up next to Harry in a sensational hornet on wheels super-bike.

"You know better than that, come on think. It looks like your wonderful imagination needs a bit of tuning up," Mark said amusingly as he shook his head at Harry.

"Oh really, is that what you think? Let's give it a try," Harry suggested.

Harry begins to think again but this time he is more focused on what he's up against. Suddenly, his machine transformed into a stunning alien-like concept vehicle and took off like a formula one race car.

He was astonished at the incredible transformation of the various machines.

"Now that's more like it," Mark emphasized.

Mark's machine quickly transformed into an incredibly stylish vehicle and flew away as quickly as a lightning bolt.

*   *   *   *   *

The training ground was a beautiful lakeside oxygenated location filled with green trees and a rich mountainous terrain within the defined horizon. The air was condensed with an unusually sweet scent.

"Mark, it smells wonderful here. What is it?" Ashley asked.

"That scent is jasmine dichotomous, or you may simply know it as jasmine. You see those white flowers along the south-east side of the lake? Those are jasmine plants. Once you start sniffing their scent, you can't seem to stop."

"I've been taking in the scent since I've arrived," Ashley said.

"Now I can see why Mark chose this location. By the way, where are you guys? I've been waiting patiently," Ashley commented.

No sooner than Ashley spoke, Mark pulled up and appeared out of a portal at the training base.

"It's about time you guys arrived," Ashley said sarcastically.

As Mark pulled up alongside Ashley's parked jet, Brian arrived followed by Harry.

They all lined their vehicles up alongside Ashley's parked jet.

"These are some amazing machines," Brian said through the communications device.

Quickly, Mark cues his team as their machines transformed into war humanoid robots.

"This training ground was designed just for this and now that we are here let's do some damage. Choose your mode to fight alone or as a team; the choice is yours," he commanded.

This gave the cue for the team to go into challenge mode, placing their machines on the medium level. The mode allowed the team to synchronize with the training ground, which quickly became swarmed with combating alien-like robots, some with flying abilities that emerged from the black glowing murky waters of a nearby lake, armed and ready to attack. The team formed a circular attack formation, but Brian was so afraid of the sight that he started to break the circle.

"What are you doing Brian?" Ashley questioned.

"Are you that unfocused? A chain is only as strong as its weakest link. Get back in here."

Brian quickly regrouped with the team, while the heinous robots continued to close in on them from all directions. Without warning, a huge alien-like creature came within arm's length of Brian.

"I guess there isn't anywhere to run to; I have this one."

Brian fired his neuro-disruptor, destroying the target. The alien blew up and disintegrated into small pieces which quickly turned into red dust, which dissolved into thin air.

"Whoa, one down. Did you see that?" Brian bragged.

Everyone was astonished. Suddenly, an unknown PA system sounded a loud continuous beep.

"Warning, you have executed a hard play!"

Mark became angry and began to chastise Brian for his execution.

"Brian, this is only training; you're not supposed to destroy the aliens."

"My mistake; I'm sorry, I'll correct it," Brian replied.

From that moment the team fought on the ground and in the air, even underwater and after two hours, the war games came to an end.

"Alright, let's wrap it up," Mark commanded.

He then deactivated the training base and the alien prototypes retreated to parts unknown.

"It appears you all have it figured out; we handled it quite well according to the report here so let's head home because we have a long day ahead of us."

The team transformed back into original concept vehicles and sped off for the underground. Everyone felt excited about this, but neither of them had an idea where this was leading to. They were loyal to Mark and believed in what he was aching to accomplish. This made him feel good, but in the back of his mind, he knew this was not going to be an easy mission to fulfill.

CHAPTER 11

ABDUCTION

It was evening, sometime around nine-thirty and the staff at Metropolitan Hospital were winding down their duties; making sure all patients had been fed, cleaned, given their medications and put to bed. After a few days, Nina was starting to become agitated with being confined to a hospital bed. Dr. Pradeep, her private physician, specifically requested that she receive lots of rest. It was late in the evening and so she was fast asleep after enjoying the company of Meghan, who lay sleeping in a chair in her room, unaware that Mark was trying to reach her from the underground laboratory.

Her forearm device which was on silent produced no sound allowing Meghan to continue to sleep peacefully. Outside in the lobby of the hospital, the nurse spoke with the physician about Nina's condition.

"I think the patient will soon be able to go home, what do you think doctor?"

"Well, according to my prognosis it appears once she's released, she'll have to be referred to a physical therapist. I would also suggest that she continues her prescribed medications. I wouldn't suggest any rigorous activity for a while until her body becomes strong again. It must have really been a powerful explosion that shook her up. Let her relax a few days more before sending her home."

It was a quiet night around the hospital and there were no patients waiting to register in the E.R. The admissions clerk was able to read a magazine while outside an armed security officer took a smoke before continuing to patrol the grounds of the hospital.

Dr. Pradeep and his nurse were the only medical examining staff on duty in the E.R that evening when, at approximately 9:45 PM, a man and a woman entered the emergency room. They approached the admissions clerk and asked to see a doctor. The clerk asked them what appeared to be the problem. The woman complained that she was suffering from gastritis.

The clerk lowered her glasses to the tip of her nostrils and scrutinized the woman to see if she was pregnant.

"Do you have medical coverage?" the clerk asked.

The woman answered yes.

"Are you pregnant?"

"No, she's not pregnant," the man answered rather abruptly.

The clerk turned her head, lowered her glasses again and scrutinized the man.

"Are you her husband?"

"Yes, I'm her husband. Can we get this over with rather quickly; my wife is in pain," the man demanded.

"Okay, as soon as you are registered then you'll be on your way. There is a doctor and a nurse on duty in the E.R this evening. Please have a little patience."

"What is your name please?"

"Ruth Medellín and this is my husband Ryan. Ryan Medellín."

"What is your religion?"

"For Christ sake, my wife is in pain. Can she see a doctor?"

The clerk then quickly finished registering the patient.

Afterwards, the clerk allowed the couple to enter a room and told them that a physician will be coming in shortly and that it was okay for the patient's husband to stay with her until the start of the examination.

It didn't take Dr. Pradeep long to arrive and start examining the patient.

"What seems to be the problem?" he asked.

"I think I ate something that's given me an upset stomach," Ruth answered quite directly as she held her stomach area.

"Is this your husband?"

"Yes."

"Mr. Medellín, would it be okay for you to wait in the lobby area for your wife. It won't take long."

"Sure doctor."

Ryan left the examining room and made his way back to the lobby area. He took a seat and browsed through his hologram device looking for any missed calls.

Meanwhile, Dr. Pradeep continued his examination.

"Okay, first I need to take your vitals."
He took the patients left arm and applied pressure to her wrist and measured her pulse. He then took out his stethoscope and measured her pulse. Afterwards, he asks her to stand so he can measure her height.

"Everything looks okay so far."

"Listen, can we get this over with I think I'm starting to feel better," Ruth rudely interjected.

"Sure, it won't take much longer."

Ruth went over to the measuring wall device and stood looking forward making eye contact with her husband, who had inconspicuously returned to the examination room. She blinked an eye at him – indicating that it was time to attack.

As the doctor approached her to measure her height, his back was fully exposed to Ryan. Without warning, he grabbed the doctor and applied a rear choke hold, cutting off his blood circulation, immediately strangling him unconscious. As he fell to the floor, Ryan lifted him up out of his white coat and carefully put it on.

"Ah, a perfect fit," he said grinning. He then put on a sterilization mask to disguise most of his face and then walked out with the patient. Together, they enter another examining room where the nurse was working with her back turned to him. This was the perfect opportunity to sneak up behind her and apply the same pressure hold executed on the doctor, which immediately knocked her out cold. Once immobilized, Ryan took off her uniform and threw it to his wife.

"Quickly, put this on."

"Come on, hurry, let's go," he says.

Together, they walked through the lobby in their disguises making their way towards the lift. Ryan then notices his device vibrating. He looks and notices that it is a video call from Nate. He knew right away that he had better answer it.

"I expected to hear from you hours ago. What are you doing? I see you've made some progress, but have you made it to the thirteenth floor yet? That's where she is."

"We're prepared and ready to enter the room of the patient. We're now boarding the lift."

"Good. Bring her to me immediately."

*　*　*　*　*

The night sky was filled with clouds and rain was just beginning to fall. There was slight thunder accompanied by a heavy gust of wind causing a power outage in the area, but the patients at the hospital were protected by the backup generators.

In the meantime, Mark continued to try to reach Meghan.

"I feel bad that I didn't fill Meghan in with everything. Things were happening so fast and I must make it up to her. I need to talk with her. I feel like there is something going on or that something's not right. I need to know this."

"She must have gone off to the hospital to visit Nina because I'm not able to track her device," Ashley indicated.

"Well, why don't we investigate?" Harry asked.

Mark listened intently and quickly felt himself going blank as if his brain had decided to shut down; but just as quickly as the feeling of numbness engulfed him, he noticed his hearing became extremely sharp and his intellect became extraordinarily great. He sensed the onset of a mutation just like those he had already experienced but this time, he felt more in control.

"Okay, then let's go! I'm ready" he said ecstatically.

*　*　*　*　*

Ryan and Ruth continued to ride the lift to the thirteenth floor. The door opened and they both exited. Ruth approached the nurse's station on the left while Ryan headed towards the patient waiting room on the right side of the lift.

"Hi, I'm trying to find the room of a patient with the last name Gates. Can you assist me?"

"Sure," the desk nurse said before looking into the computer to find that information.

"The patient is in room 1313. She's on medication and may need to continue to rest. Are you administered to give her care?"

"No, I was only assigned to monitor her sleep-wake cycle just for the night."

Ruth then turned and walked toward the area where Ryan awaited her.

"She's in room 1310. Let's go."

"I'll take it from here, wait for me."

Ruth sat down in a chair outside the room, while Ryan stood at the door, looked through the glass pane and observed both Nina and Meghan fast asleep. Slowly, he took out his neuro-disruptor from underneath his white coat and opened the door. He quickly rushed in and pointed his weapon at Nina, gradually raising it to fire but then Meghan woke just in time to knock it from his hands. She screamed for help, as Ruth entered, seeing her wrestling with Ryan on the floor.

"Someone called for help?" Ruth asked.

"Shoot her now!" Ryan yelled.

Meghan quickly rolls to one side and goes after Ryan's weapon as Ruth opens fire with a tranquillizer gun, hitting Meghan in the torso. This shuts down her nervous system, thus restricting her from firing the retrieved neuro-disruptor. Soon afterwards Nina opens her eyes, but Ruth stuns her with a shock from her tranquillizer gun.

"Never send a man to do a woman's job, let's get them out of here," Ruth says as she looks down at Ryan. He activates his forearm bracelet and in no time a craft hovers next to the window. Ruth opens it and the hospital's security alarm system goes off.

Outside, the desk nurse hears the commotion, runs into the room and screams before running back to her desk to call the security officer. Right away, the officer immediately deactivates the lift system, thus minimalizing a means of escape.

Quickly Ryan and Ruth load the bodies in the hovering craft outside of the window. The desk nurse and the hospital security guard are the first to rush toward the room, as the UIO make their way up the stairs towards the thirteenth floor. They exit the stairwell and make way towards the hospital room. Within a few meters of the room, they spot Ryan and give him a warning to drop his weapon.

Ruth and her hostages are about to exit the window onto a waiting craft when suddenly, the officers open fire and in return, Ryan fires his neuro-disruptor hitting one of the officers twice in the abdomen leaving holes going through him.

"Animals," Ryan yells.

*   *   *   *   *

132

At that very moment, Mark, Ashley, Brian, and Harry arrive in Mark's Tungsten QX12, and exit the vehicle in the parking lot of the hospital. Suddenly they look up and watch as Ruth and Ryan depart with Nina and Meghan.

"What is going on here. Looks like Meghan and Nina are both being kidnapped, oh my God!"

Harry and Mark can't believe what they are seeing.

They appear to be in shock and stand transfixed. Harry had purchased two dozen roses for Nina but suddenly they drop from his hand to the ground.

"No!" Mark yells.

Mark quickly takes out his gun, switches the mode, aims, and fires a tracking device onto the craft as it glides away.

It was only a moment later that Mark received a call from Meghan's device. He knew something was awfully wrong. He let the device ring one time and contemplated whether to answer it or not.

On the second ring, he stared at the device and silently prayed that Meghan was okay. On the third ring, he became tense and activated his earpiece to answer the call. He listened to the voice on the other end without saying a word.

There was heavy breathing for a few seconds. Then a voice, sort of raspy, slightly mechanical, and somewhat sinister started to relay a message.

"I know you can hear me, so you see, I'm just going to keep taking them one by one until you hand over the substance to me."

Mark knew right away that it was Nate on the device.

"I should've known," Mark said.

"But don't you worry. I'll find you, and when I do, I'll annihilate you."

"Oh, how clever of you," Nate responded and hung up the device.

Mark turned to his crew and gave a command.

"Alright, time to gear up. We have a mission to accomplish."

With the use of their fore-arm devices, Ashley, Brian, Harry, and Mark immediately activated their machines which were parked in Mark's underground laboratory.

In no time, the machines autonomously transported themselves through the tunnel, straight to the parking area of the hospital. The car park was slightly empty, and the crew was able to enter their crafts inconspicuously. They then manoeuvred in an acute angle with Mark in the lead and they followed him according to the tracking device on their digital display screens inside their craft.

As they flew stealth mode over the luscious green mountains below, Mark ingeniously led his team on the start of a mission, hoping to succeed in stopping Nate.

"Okay, I have the target on screen!" Mark confirmed.

Without warning, a group of four flying war machines, pale against the grim night sky, dropped from the atmosphere into a stealth position, hovering five kilometres away, and facing in the direction of Mark's team.

As Mark looked out into the distance observing the craft, his power allowed him to zoom in on the pilots who had faces that resembled wasps with eyes of shiny black fire. No other member of the team was given this privilege. Then mysteriously, one of the alien machines erupted and transformed into a chariot of fire with the alien-like pilot at the helm, riding a pale horse with flaming hair, resembling Satan. Just that quick the chariot transformed back into a pale machine hovering along with the others.

Without warning, they slowly started gliding towards Mark and his crew. It was obvious that the crew was astonished and had never experienced anything like what they were experiencing now. Nonetheless, they continued to fly in the direction of the four machines.

It was obvious that they were preparing to attack. Mark could tell right away that these four beasts were sent by Nate and were given the power to initiate earth's destruction.

Without warning, the pale alien craft took off and sped in the direction towards Mark.

"It's coming right at us, buckle up," he stated.

"Oh God, what do I do?" Brian shouted nervously.

"If you never in your life prayed before, now is the time to do so," Mark replied.

"Whatever you do stay alert until its time. Here we go."

Meanwhile, Nate sat and watched the action unfold from a secret room in his facility.

"This should confuse them a bit; I need that substance," he said vehemently.

He then continued to watch the action as his war machines closed in on Mark and his crew. As they dodged the attack, they alternately returned the fire; Mark fired missiles meant to destroy one of three machines, while the other two machines attacked him from opposite angles.

Just as quickly as he believed he destroyed the pale machine; Mark witnesses a terrifying metamorphosis.

The forms a small mushroom cloud, which then turns into a giant cloud and quickly descends forming snow, sleet, and hail over the land. The strange precipitation suddenly stopped to the amazement of both sides.

Then suddenly, a gust of wind swirled the accumulated precipitation around until it formed a giant ice-crystal Lipizzaner stallion with a magnificent mane and wings resembling Pegasus. But what was extraordinary is that its brilliant white colour slowly began to fade and after a moment it changed and became fiery red, its mane resembled a blazing fire, and its eyes were those of a serpent. It knocked its hoofs against the ground making a loud noise which was then softened by the strong wind. Mark noticed its hoofs were cloven with ice, gold, diamonds, sapphires, and semi-precious jewels and it stood, silently as if it were a gift from the gods.

"Do you see what just happened?" Ashley asked.

"Let's split up," Mark suggested as he spoke through his earpiece.

"Whatever this thing is, it's pretty powerful; let's be careful out here. These guys have some tricks underneath their sleeves. I'll stay with this red one, while you go after the other three."

The team split up quickly as they individually chased and battled it out with the other war machines.

"Man, whatever they are, they're quite fast," Harry said.

A flying machine shoots a laser rapidly while chasing Harry through the sky. Another tries to head him off by speeding past him and making a loop, coming right back-full force-in his direction. Harry then quickly destroys the opposing machine.

"One down, at least for now," he pointed out.

But what he doesn't realize is that the secret of these alien-like machines is they have the power to regenerate three times before they die.

"Egad," Nate exclaims from his facility.

"I refuse to be defeated by mere mortals, get rid of those puny humans."

Mark hovers his craft in the direction of the giant red Pegasus who sits motionless like the Trojan horse, as if awaiting something or someone. Suddenly, a lightning bolt strikes it and as if by magic a rider appears on the horse's back, pulls the rein attached to the bit, then whips the magnificent beast with a bolt of lightning, causing it to execute a courbette on his hind legs, and with each hop, it shook the earth around him; while simultaneously flapping its powerful wings, neighing loudly and causing thunder to roar across the sky. The wind around it is howled loudly and the pressure alone from the flapping of its huge wings caused Mark's machine to become unstable and go out of control. But something eerie transcends this scene. The rider's face is aflame; his head is covered by a red hooded cape which reaches all the way down, sweeping the Earth, and spreading plague amongst the people. On his right hip, he brandished a great sword tied to a chain that had the embedded words *Dolore Sanguinem Belli*, which were Latin for *Agony, Blood, and War*. He then declared silence and relayed his message in a loud voice.

"Dolore, Sanguinem, Belli, Dolore, Sanguinem, Belli, Dolore, Sanguinem, Belli."

The rider then turned toward Mark and delivered his message, but before all of this, the powerful force of the horse's flapping wings briefly disabled all video feed to Nate. There followed an eerie silence.

The rider then spoke in a loud mechanical voice;

"Though I was sent to destroy mankind, I sympathize with your cause. You are in grave danger. Your mission here is known and powerful enemies are preparing to destroy you."

Suddenly, the red horse changed colours to cloud grey, then neighed loudly causing thunder in great waves of discordant and demented sounds. The noise level became so intense that it made Mark tremble. The wind raised to the level of a thousand howling hounds. No one dared to speak, because fear transformed intelligible words into agonizing moans and groans.

Seconds later, without warning, it flew off into the air, as fast as lighting and disappeared into the heavens.

Meanwhile, the rest of the crew was battling the alien crafts.

"Guys, I can't shake this thing!" Ashley said screaming through her earpiece.

"Use your invisible shield," Mark replied. Ashley takes Mark's suggestion and thinks about invisibility and instantly her thoughts trigger her craft to disappear into thin air, leaving the opposing machine baffled. This allowed her to close in on the war machine, undetected, in preparation for causing its destruction.

Again, Nate can see streaming visuals of the action. However, he becomes angry and jumps out of his seat, pounding the table.

"Where the hell did it disappear?" he said referring to Ashley's machine.

"Hello, I see you, but you can't see me!" she jested.

She then aims and fires and in one shot destroys the target. Nate is in disbelief as his visual perception becomes grated out. Upset, he turns away from the screen and shouts, "Useless pieces of nothingness."

He then turns towards his wingman Chase and gives him a command, pounding his fist on the table all at the same time.

"I want you to find them and annihilate them," he exclaims pointing his finger.

"And this time, send in the humanoids."

The craft with the tracking device quickly flew away but Mark and the team scrupulously follows.

"Guys, whatever you do, please don't destroy it; there are valuables inside," Mark urged.

The team watches the navigation on the screen while keeping a live visual of the craft at a distance when without warning it explodes wiping out the tracking signals and the hostages that it contained.

"No," Mark cries in agony, as bits and pieces of the craft descend to the ground like snowflakes. The team is shocked at the site of the explosion, seconds later a visual of Nate appears on Mark's screen.

"I warned you, now if you don't mind, I have business to attend to," Nate says ferociously.

"No," Mark yells in disbelief as Nate intrudes on his display screens. Furious, Mark loses control of his craft but quickly regains it after taking the necessary precautions.

The video streaming ends and the team quickly lands their machines to investigate the area where the craft carrying Nina, Meghan, Ryan, and Ruth exploded. The team spreads out into different areas to make the search more effective. Not long after searching the area Ashley spots one of Meghan's earrings. Nervously, she hurries over and picks it up while the team observes other areas.

"Oh no, guys come and look," she vexed.

Without a word, the rest of the team walked over to Ashley and she shows them one of the earrings that Meghan wore. Mark takes the earring and holds it in his right hand closes his fist and shakes his head in anguish and disbelief, not wanting to release his true feelings; he wonders how to handle the situation.

"God, what have I done?" he cries out.

CHAPTER 12

RUN FOR COVER

ark was feeling quite melancholy and found it rather difficult to contain his emotions. He was obviously distraught over the thought of his beautiful Meghan and Nina being lifeless and he felt he was to blame.

"This whole thing is my fault," he moaned holding his head in shame, shaking it from side to side. It was obvious that right now he was a broken man and his spirit was quite low.

"Don't say that Mark. It's not your fault," Ashley said as she walked over to him and placed her hand on his shoulder.

"I did say it, it is my fault, yet I'm trying to be optimistic and in doing so I think they must be alive somewhere because there are no bodies to prove they're dead. This can't be right. That fiend Nate must be playing with us to make us believe they're dead so I could hand over the novaerium to him"

Harry looked perplexed and questioned Mark's comment.

"What do you mean he just blew up the..."

Mark quickly interrupts Harry before he finishes his comment.

"No, that's not how it happened."

Brian then turned to Mark in disbelief and said, "Man, are you blind or something? Look around you. There's debris from the explosion all over the place. Didn't you see what just happened here?"

Everyone looked around again to make sure there was not anything that was overlooked. The ground didn't seem to change much from the last time they scrutinized it. This all seemed like a waste of time to the team, but they didn't want to disrespect Mark.

"Well, what are we going to do now?" Ashley asked.

There seemed to be a deafening silence as everyone looked around at one another as if they were looking for one of them to provide an answer. There was nothing but silence and an occasional gust of wind. Mark knew he had to say something that would continue to secure his leadership with the team.

He knew he had to think of something fast, but his thoughts were interrupted by a crackle of thunder as black clouds sprawled across the sky. Their brassy glare drained color from the surrounding area leaving blank faces tinted bronze in the faltering light.

Mark stood motionless as the scent of rain grew dark and heavy. A stillness fell over the night, and in the moment of silence came a second crackle of thunder followed by the pattering of tiny raindrops. For a moment, everything stopped. Even the wind seemed to hold its breath. Then suddenly, a streak of lightning split the sky, and the downpour began.

Mark finally knew he had to speak.

"No; we wait, this is probably one of Nate's dirty little tricks," he suggested to the team.

Harry wasn't sure if this was the right thing to do.

"Wait? Are you certain we should wait?" he asked wiping the rain from his forehead.

"Yes, wait," Mark assured him.

"They have what I need, and I have what they want."

Harry looked at Mark and replied, "Why you bloody selfish human being."

He then walked over to him and punched him in the face. The impact caused Mark to fall back but he was able to stay on his feet. Mark was baffled by this and in disbelief.

"Have you lost your mind, they're all dead!" Harry exclaimed.

He then turned and walked away towards his craft. The door to the craft was approximately 2.1 meters away but to Harry, it seemed like a long stretch in the pouring rain. He had a lot of thoughts running through his mind and taking over the leadership of this mission was one of them, especially when it came to the thought of Nina. He wasn't going to sit around and wait for Mark to decide on what they should or shouldn't do. It was obvious he was angry, and it showed in the action he previously displayed.

A crackle of lightning flashed, and loud thunder was heard over-head.

"I'll find Nate and kill him myself," he cried menacingly.

At that moment Mark ran over to Harry and tripped him up and they began wrestling on the wet sandy ground. They both contend to battle one another in a pacified combat. It was obvious they didn't want to hurt one another but instead, just wanted to let off some steam.

"You're crazy, your thoughts are going to get us all killed," Mark accused Harry before landing a punch to his abdomen. Harry absorbed the punch but reciprocated with a knee kick to Mark's left rib cage which caused him to lose his momentum. He then quickly followed up with a punch towards the face, but Mark's quick reflex blocked it.

"I don't want to do battle with you Harry," Mark exclaimed thus pushing him over and rolling atop of him and pinning him down.

"Get the bloody hell off me," Harry said as he tried to wriggle his way out of the hold.

Mark secured his hold atop of him by strengthening his grip around his opponents neck and thoracic cavity.

While all this fighting was taking place, Ashley spotted two alien warcraft off in the distance approaching at top speed. Without warning the danger approached unannounced by the radar detection device.

"Oh no, this can't be good," Ashley stated as the warcraft approached.

Brian also saw them approaching. As they closed in, the crew realized that they were war machines coming from Nate's arsenal.

"Run for cover. We're all going to be doomed!"

Mark and Harry immediately came to a halt and jumped to their feet to observe the approaching menace.

A loud thunderbolt jolted the sky as the four of them stood motionless and tense with only seconds left to decide their next manoeuvre. All at once, an arsenal appeared out of nowhere which caused them to dive into the sand for cover with their hands on their head. Seconds later the warcraft came to a hover over the ground near Mark and his team. The warcraft then released a blue gel-like blob that fell to the ground before quietly flying off. After it left, the team stood up and looked around astounded to notice that they were not ambushed. Unaware of the substance, Ashley cautiously went back to check out the blob, but Mark stopped her in her tracks.

"Wait, that's not safe, stand back," he advised them.

Mark took off a sneer from the body of his suit; activated it from his forearm device and threw it at the gel to scan for radiation. The sneer hovered around the blob in a circular motion, while collecting data.

He observed that the substance contained a nucleus within its centre and after scrutinizing the data imaging from his forearm device he notices that an object within the nucleus resembled a human fetus. Immediately, he activates the electrocardiogram within the forearm device, which detected that there was no heartbeat.

"What do you think?" Ashley asked curiously.

"Well, let's dissect this and see what's in it," Mark replied.

"Okay team, we should all stand back because I don't want this stuff popping out all over your Sunday best."

He then activates the sneer to cut the substance open. Again, the sneer performs a series of observatory flights around the dimensions of the object before using a laser to snip away at its circumference. As the object began to open everyone noticed an opaque viscous fluid starting to ooze out of the blob. But even more ominous was the glowing green light within the nucleus of this substance, which became brighter and brighter as it opened.

It took several minutes for the sneer laser to penetrate the blob as it neared completion of its task. Suddenly, as the blob opened, the body of a tortured man resembling Domonic, immersed in this blue yolk-like substance, fell out onto the sand as if a woman had just given birth to a stillborn child.

Like quicksilver, Mark reminisced to the time when he first encountered the novaerium. His thoughts took him back to when the purple gaseous bubble of the novaerium burst throwing a small amount of fluid onto his forearm, which then released a powerful chemical which rushed into his bloodstream causing physiological mutations and psychological hallucinations. This caused a flashing of the universe in his head as his body began to shake uncontrollably. This horrified Ashley as she screamed in terror and nearly fainted. Everyone gasped at what they saw. Ashley's scream caused Mark to quickly snap out of this dream state.

"Oh no," Ashley sighed as she placed her head on Brian's shoulder and cried. Within seconds Brian felt her limp body and he struggled to hold her up.

"Hey, guys, Ashley has fainted."

Overcome with grief, sadness, and terror, Mark walked over to the blue slimy body; he kneeled and took a good look before confirming his fear that it is Domonic. "I've had enough," he wailed.

* * * * *

It's about 6:10 AM in the mountainous desert and the heavy rain has subsided. Ashley regained her energy and was back in action with the team, and together they dug three graves to accommodate the expired body of Domonic, and what they thought were the ashes of Meghan and Nina. As Mark loaded Meghan's ashes into one grave, Harry loaded Nina's into another. They followed this with a moment of silence before covering them with sand. Mark and Harry then placed the symbols of Nina and Meghan on their graves. Mark took a deep breath as he looked down onto upon them.

He lamented by shaking his head, still not able to come to the realization of what was happening right before his very eyes.

Next, Harry and Mark carefully loaded Domonic's limp body into a third grave. They followed this with a moment of silence before starting to cover the grave with wet sand. Suddenly, Harry gasped in astonishment as Domonic's limp body seemed to show signs of life.

"I think he's alive!" he yells uncontrollably.

Astonished, Mark jumped back and looked at Domonic's pulsating body.

"Yes, he is alive and he's moving. Let's get him out of there quickly."

Ashley was in total shock and disbelief as Mark and Harry began to lift Domonic out of his grave, placing his limp body on the wet ground. While lying there, Domonic coughs up sputum but was still unaware of his surroundings. Slowly awakening from his ordeal, yet filled with adrenaline, he senses danger and attempts to reach for Mark's gun to defend himself.

"What is he doing, keep him down. He's aimless like some wild beast. He's acting quite strange," Harry said while trembling.

"Hey Mark, what is this guy doing? He's totally out of control. Hey, wait a minute," Brian said still with the gun aimed at Domonic.

Suddenly, streaks of pure white crackled against a stormy blanket of grey clouds, thus bursting them open and allowing the rain to fall freely.

Mark and Harry held Domonic down for his own safety as he tried to wrestle out of the hold. Out of nowhere, he seemed to have acquired superhuman strength.

"Hey man, calm down. I'm your brother, you're safe with me," Mark stated.

"Let's get him inside out of the rain and get some aid for him right now."

They each take him by a shoulder and bring him into an area where they were able to put up a tent and he was able to rest comfortably.

"I don't know if you can hear me or comprehend what I'm saying, but I just want you to know that I love you very much and hope you get better soon," Ashley assured Domonic with tears in her eyes as she smoothed his hair atop his head.

She then prepared to give him first aid by slowly cutting off his wet clothes and checking to see if he had any wounds.

"I must say that seeing you again is truly something special," she says, smiling down and looking into his blank pale face. As she continued to examine him she noticed a bullet wound that looked as if it needed attention.

"This is terrible," she said as the rain beat against the outside of the tent.

She reaches and hands Domonic a blanket that was brought in from the craft to keep him warm, while she dresses the wounds, before going out to see Mark who is attending other business.

"Ashley, what appears to be the problem? Is everything okay with my brother? He's lucky to have you. What's going on?"

Ashley looked at Mark and he notices that something was wrong.

She looks down and then looks him straight in the eyes.

"He's not looking so good, there seems to be an open wound that's making him worst by the second and so he doesn't have much time."

Mark looks at her in disbelief.

"I must see this."

They go back in to look at Domonic. His condition seems to be intense and indeed he appears to be in a slight coma and not completely in control of his faculties.

"He looks like he's out of touch with reality. It's as if he is in a dream state. Get him to the underground laboratory immediately, there you'll be able to better assist him. We have some retaliating to do. I'm going to kick Nate's arse," Mark says angrily.

"Be careful you guys," Ashley told them before they left.

"Don't worry about us. We can take care of ourselves."

"Okay, I'll leave that in your hands," Ashley says as she prepares to fly Domonic to the laboratory for treatment.

Meanwhile, Mark and his crew prepare to fly out towards Nate's facility.

"Alright, team let's do this. We're going to finish this guy once and for all. We're going to destroy everything at his facility."

Mark was determined, more than ever, to take Nate down. But little did he know that at this very moment, Nate was already ahead of him, having planned an attack of his own and had a surprise in store for Mark and his entire team.

Nate had secretly planted a nanochip in Domonic's left hand. This tiny chip had a recording and a tracking device along with an electromagnetic pulse, strong enough to knock a human body out completely. It allowed Nate to gather data on Domonic as well as pick up radio frequencies enabling him to occasionally listen to a conversation but more than anything else, it afforded him the ability to track movement.

Meanwhile, at his facility, Nate walked over to four standing glass tubes filled with a red fluid which held the bodies of Meghan and Nina. Their heads were covered with filtered masks. Nate looked at the encapsulated bodies, moved in closer to the tubes, and touched each of them as if he was caressing an old girlfriend.

"It won't be long now," he growled before letting out a menacing grin.

He was then approached by Serena, a tall slender blonde robot, who was his administrative assistant. She walked up to him and delivered a message.

"Your transportation is ready sir," she says.

He gestures her with an okay hand, then continued to round up a team of humanoids, who board a warcraft and take off for Mark's laboratory.

At the very same time, Mark and his team arrive at Nate's facility. Upon arrival, their crafts transformed into camouflage invisible human-size robots. They notice that the building is surrounded by Nate's soldiers. Mark can see them from a distance positioned all over and securing the area. To get inside, Mark, Harry, and Brian slowly overtake Nate's forces. This gives them the edge to move further in taking control of the facility.

Off in the distance, a huge flying machine hovers over Mark's diner making a loud sound. It followed the nanochip's GPS just outside of the bar and grill until the signal dropped. From the craft, Nate looked down at the location where the signal was lost.

"The only way that the signal could have dropped is if this guy is underground or surrounded by a force field of some sort."

"But wait a minute. This is where I last tracked it. It must be here."

The powerful winds from the warcraft engine blowed free-standing objects around as it landed. Nate signaled the soldiers to patrol the perimeter of the area, but to no avail; they are unable to find any signs of what Nate is looking for and report back to him that all is clear. This puzzles him as he returns to the craft.

"I can't imagine why we're not able to detect him. Where is he? Perhaps he found the chip and destroyed it," Chase stated.

"Impossible. How could that be? He couldn't have because he doesn't know it's planted inside of him. There must be more to this; perhaps some form of intelligence has interrupted my plans," Nate whined frantically.

Suddenly, he became angry and circumvents by performing a tantrum. He sounds a command and all the soldiers return to the craft. The warcraft starts up and in a matter of seconds, it takes off. As it spins in the air, it makes a couple of manoeuvres then, without warning, it aims its laser directly at the bar and grill and blows it to pieces.

CHAPTER 13

13 SARCOPHAGI RED TUBES

From within the underground laboratory, Domonic felt the explosion above. It rattled the entire building causing it to become unstable. It woke him from his dream state, where he went through a series of flashbacks of what took place while he was captured, tortured, and shot. He was also able to foresee Nate destroying the bar and grill. It was a ghastly, horrible scene. Seconds later, his body pouring with sweat, started to shake uncontrollably. He found himself gasping for air, which caused him to jump up into a sitting position as sweat poured down his head. Ashley sat close by and comforted him. He sat on the edge of the bed and she reached for a glass of water and passed it to him. He took a drink and then attempted to figure out the events that transpired during his dream, yet he couldn't quite put it all together.

Meanwhile, chaos erupted everywhere during which time Mark and his team arrived in the central location of Nate's laboratory where another set of humanoids were in position waiting to attack. After the team entered the room, they immediately began executing their targets with the help of camouflage warfare. The fighting grew intense with both sides suffering casualties.

"I'm hit," Harry shouted as he dropped to his knees. It was obvious that he was feeling excruciating pain, but he was still alert.

"Brian, I'm hit. It's serious. Help me!" he cried out.

Nevertheless, he continued to fire his neuro-disruptor at the enemy forces. Brian looked in his direction and saw that he needed help. He quickly rushed over to cover and assist him. Blood was oozing from his leg.

"Hey bud, you're bleeding. Let me help you."

Brian activated nanobots to perform medical procedures inside Harry's bodies. In the meantime he took out gauze from his first aid kit, attached to his unique space suit, and wrapped the wound tightly. After he dressed it, he prayed that things will get better.

"There, you're lucky, it could be worst."

"Crazy aliens, they tried to kill me," Harry groaned in pain.

"Yeah, they're crazy but we're just as crazy to try to fight these aliens."

Harry gave Brian a puzzling look as if he was speaking a foreign language.

"Come on bud. Get back on your feet and let's do this."

Harry and Brian then positioned themselves back to back to take out the enemy targets as they attempted to move closer towards a neutral location that would put them out of harm's way.

Not far off in the distance, Mark noticed a bright red light, which appeared to glow like a giant alien spacecraft. He stared as its beams involuntarily stopped him in his tracks. Its rays had him in a state of suspended animation. He was transfixed by its illumination and was motionless, even while all the fighting was taking place around him.

Suddenly, the fighting halted, and the other members of his team also became motionless and stared at the strange red glowing lights beaming on and off in the distance.

Curiosity overtook Mark as he slowly walked in the direction of the brightness. He knew it was dangerous to go ahead without the cover of his team, but he had his weapons in case of danger.

As he slowly proceeded along in hopes of finding new evidence, which might show whether Meghan and Nina were dead or alive, he couldn't help to think that this illumination would lead him to an answer. As he edged closer, he came to an open laboratory with giant test tubes filled with a bubbling iridescent viscous red fluid, resembling human blood plasma, with wires attached to the top exterior of the tubes. The fluid appeared to be boiling inside but it was obvious to notice that the volume rate of flow was inversely proportional to the viscosity, as might be expected. Mark knew that it is evident from the general nature of viscous effects that the velocity of a viscous fluid flowing through a tube will not be the same at all points within the tube. The flow within appeared to be stable; yet there was hardly any.

The tubes, numbered one through thirteen, were large enough to hold a human body, like glass sarcophagi, and were the kind used in body cooling experiments.

Mark marvelled at the vision before him and moved closer to inspect them. He scrutinized each tube and its contents slowly. Suddenly, he came to the fourth and fifth tube and realized that there was something or someone inside each one that looked like mummies. It appeared that the outermost layer of fluid seemed to cling to the wall of the tube and its velocity was zero.

As he pressed his face against the tube and peered closer, he was assured that inside rest the bodies of Meghan and Nina floating in suspended animation. Astonished, he patted the circumference of the entire tube in search of an opening. As he did they began to glow, and he was able to see their dimensions. He was able to estimate its width and hypothesized that they appeared to be made from a thick polymer glass-like material.

He observed that each tube had a chart with exponential terms written on them. As he inched closer, he noticed a cloud of red steam hovering over each of the tubes and an electrical shock wave that was frequently generated every few seconds from the exterior wire attachments that travelled down the wire through the tube's interior, to a helmet attached on the head of each body. Mark was in disbelief.

"What in heaven's name is this?" he muttered to himself.

"What kind of place is this?"

While in his moment of shock, Mark didn't notice that he was being surrounded by Ricardo, Chase, and Ruth who appeared out of nowhere. They pointed their neuro-disruptors at him from three different angles. Suddenly, Mark tried to reach for his weapon but realized that he was outnumbered.

"I wouldn't'' do that if I were you," Ricardo belted out.

"Drop your weapon and put your hands high in the air," Ruth demanded.

Mark dropped his weapon and held up his hands. Ruth then went over and picked up his neuro-disruptor from the ground.

"You really think you can just enter into our domain and do as you please? I'm sorry to say it just doesn't work that way," Ricardo stated.

"Detain him now!"

Chase immediately overpowered Mark, in an attempt to restrain him, but as Mark's anticipation built up and with Ruth's neuro-disruptor pointed at him, just centimetres away; he skillfully yanked the weapon from her and takes her hostage with it pointed at her head. Helpless, she screams for someone to help get her out of this perilous position. She struggles in the beginning but then sees there is no use to continue.

"Any closer and I'll kill her," Mark says to Chase and Ricardo.

"I don't think I need to tell you to lower your weapons," Mark said fearlessly as he pointed his neuro-disruptor at Ruth's head, pressing the nozzle into her skull. Ricardo and Chase slowly lower their weapons, but Ricardo hesitates.

In the same vein, Harry and Brian were secretly spying on the whole chain of events and were making their way towards the action. Now in position, they both aim and shoot at their targets hitting Chase in the chest sending him flying backwards, knocking him out against a polymer glass tube, while another beam hits Ricardo in his lower extremities.

Ricardo then conjures up the strength to raise his weapon and fires at the head of Ruth but misses. He then fired again at Mark but missed him by only a few centimetres. Not wanting to remain in this predicament, Ricardo runs for cover, but not before shooting the tube holding Nina and taking her hostage. The red viscous chemical leaks out all over partially covering the floor.

Ricardo gawped at Mark and said, "You'll have to kill her before you get to me."

He slowly backs up, throwing her drenched body into a polymer transport mechanism, and quickly escapes through the tunnel.

Amid all the commotion, Brian and Harry arrive and were surprised to see the huge tube with Meghan floating in suspended animation and the other broken tube without a body in sight. Brian carefully stepped over the red viscous fluid on the floor and turned towards Mark.

"What happened here?"

"Ricardo broke the tube and took Nina."

"Wait, my Nina, she is still alive?" Harry asked speculatively.

He then turned and furiously began to search for Ricardo, while Brian went over to check Chase's pulse to see if he was still alive or dead.

*　*　*　*　*

Back at the underground, wearing only sweatpants and exposing a bandaged muscular torso, Domonic curiously made his way through a tunnel which led to a ladder leading up to a manhole, which opened onto the street. He scrupulously climbed the ladder to the manhole, partially lifted off the cylinder cover and peered through to the outside. He observed an enemy craft and soldiers upon which he quickly closed the cylinder and scurried back down the ladder to the underground area to update Ashley.

Suddenly, an explosion blew off the cylinder.

"Come on we have to get out of here; hurry!" Domonic said nervously.

Moving rather quickly, he puts on a leather jacket and along with Ashley, they both head for the vehicle. Seconds later, Nate and his team arrive at the laboratory where they encounter Domonic and Ashley about to take off.

Inside the vehicle, Domonic revs the engine in preparation to speed away from the lab through the underground tunnel. Nate looked at him surprisingly and grinned.

"Leaving so soon, you won't make it far with that bug inserted in your arm."

He then turned on a device which executes an electric shock to Domonic as he tries to take off; the shock paralyzes him, and he loses control sending his vehicle crashing into the wall of the laboratory, opening a hole big enough for Nate to walk in with ease.

"You all make it so pathetically easy for me," Nate confessed.

He and his team then begin to search for the novaerium throughout the laboratory.

While all of this is taking place, Mark captured Ruth and takes her as a hostage. Securing her in a sleeping pod in his machine, he then walks over to the tube that is holding Meghan and pushes a button that drains the viscous substance and slowly opens the thick glass door. He takes her out and holds her wet body in his arms and with her eyes closed, he touches her face.

She doesn't respond but he notices that her face is well preserved.

"Glad to see you both back together again," Brian inserted.

Mark turned to Brian and smiled. He was able to see the humiliation Brian showed on his face yet they both were determined to get this whole thing over with. He then quickly turns back to Meghan and looks at her. He touches her wet hair. He looks around the laboratory and spots a dried cloth napkin.

"Brian, get me that towel from off the lab table and hurry," he says. Brian quickly retrieves the towel and brings it over to Mark.

He begins to dry her face. In his mind he can only wonder what she had gone through. He knew that it will take a bit of time to solve this puzzle and that he should proceed cautiously in destroying Nate and his crew. He knew that he had to think and plan to cut him down. He had already made up his mind that he won't stop until Nate was no more. He had no other choice in the matter but to continue with his mission.

*　*　*　*　*

Nate was fascinated with Mark's laboratory. As he rambled through cabinets, files, papers, chemical supplies and other unprecedented places, he finally came across something that excites his attention.

"Eureka! I've found it!" he shouts.

The portion of the novaerium, about 15 ml, was a small amount but it was enough to give Nate power to build a machine that would control the world.

Completely overjoyed, he turned towards the crashed vehicle as it exudes a ghostly array of smoke in the corner of the lab.

"Finally, after all these years the search is over, and the world will be mine," Nate conjured.

He then let out a disturbing grin as he thought of his conspiracy to take control of the world.

Outside, there was a loud haunting cheer that came from his crew, as they performed a victory dance, jumping and stomping the ground like savages.

Not far away, Mark was getting prepared to take out Nate and his men.

Suddenly, Ashley radioed in.

"Mark, are you there, Mark, come in."

"Yes, go ahead."

"Nate has the novaerium."

"This can't be; how did this happen?"

"I don't know, somehow he destroyed the diner and broke into the laboratory."

"Are you okay Ashley?"

"Yes, we're okay. There was a crash. I was able to get out, but I fear for Domonic; even though his accident protection foam was activated along with mine, he's still stuck inside the vehicle."

"Alright, stay put. I'll be right there."

At that moment, Harry returned from chasing after Ricardo. He was not satisfied because he expected to capture him and stop him completely.

"That creep has my girl. We have to find him, he escaped," Harry belted out.

"I can see that," Brian replied.

"Listen, you two, we have a bigger problem at hand."

"What on earth are you talking about?" Harry asked quite puzzled.

"The novaerium; Nate has found it and taken it."

Harry and Brian were both struck with awe at the news.

"I thought you had it secured where no one else could get a hold of this thing. What happened?" Harry asked inquisitively.

"That was true up until now. Somehow, he broke into my laboratory. I'm puzzled how that ever happened. No one was supposed to be able to get inside?"

*   *   *   *   *

Off in a subunit hidden laboratory in the desert, Nate measures out a portion of the novaerium, which he doesn't know by name but assumedly thinks he will eventually be able to call it *natetonium* and claim it as his

own discovery. Nonetheless, he measures a portion to use for putting together a powerful army of war humanoids, each charged with the chemical, to battle Mark's team while he goes off throughout the universe seeking more strength from various intergalactic criminal powers. However, despite his dream of universal imperialism, Nate is annoyed as to how his plans to also use the novaerium to help power the *Mosquito*, a micro-electromechanical programmable hexapod agent code-named *Arevun*, to gather data on sources of thermonuclear hydrogen use by major corporations was ever exposed.

Nate had planned to use the novaerium to give this hexapod the ability to fly and manoeuvre just like a flying insect but with the perception, navigation, and intelligence of a machine. Nate planned to program this undetectable flying hexapod, to migrate long distances to crack codes and infiltrate the security systems of governments and major corporations. Once entrance is gained, a single *Arevun* would then divide itself into several micro-hexapods.

This new army of undetectable hexapods would then combine advanced analytical thinking and position themselves in high-level areas within the brain of these corporations and governments, where each would then use an extended proboscis to insert into the main frame of a computer to take nano-size pictures of data from the file of the computer before transforming back into a single *Arevun*, whose lifelong function is to transmit the information via satellite back to Nate's IT team aboard his spaceship before disappearing into the fourth dimension.

He was even more angered that his plans to wreak havoc on Earth were exposed and he wanted to find out why and how his plans were leaked. His goal was to attack the seven continents and proclaim his authority to the world in a secret message which he code-named *The Seventh Seal*. His overall goal was to disrupt the diplomatic functions of the United Nations, kidnap the world leaders of its member countries and force their governments to cooperate with his plans to destroy humanity.

"I will create a new world order and I will become its supreme leader," he affirmed.

* * * * *

The humanoids continued to patrol Nate's laboratory as he conceived ideas of how to use the novaerium to his advantage.

171

About 1.6 kilometers away from Nate's facility, Mark and his team continued their plan to stop Nate.

"Here are some of the things that I failed to show you back at the laboratory," Mark said to his team. He then pulls up a display of what could happen if novaerium is used incorrectly.

Brian looks over the information, then turns and looked at Harry to see his expression.

"And you mean to tell us that some psychotic maniac is running around with that thing? You should have told us about this novaerium a long time ago," Brian stressed.

"I thought I had it under control; with all the safety mechanisms in place, this should have never happened."

"So how do we stop this guy?" Harry asked.

Mark looked at him and pondered. He then walked over to a section of the desert area and initiated a feature on his forearm device.

"The possibilities of what could happen with the power of the novaerium are endless and with his intentions, who knows what he is capable of doing," Mark explained.

"One obnoxious man with all that power," Brian inserts.

"And not just any power. We are talking about the power that could put an end to humanity."

Brian looked at Mark in disbelief that all of this was really happening. He looked up at the stars over the desert before looking back at Mark and replied.

"So, we better be well prepared."

Mark seemed to be in deep thought.

"First we have to find him."

He then activated four snares to locate the energy of the novaerium.

"This will help find the source and as soon as it does, we attack."

Each snare swiftly went out in search of data including visuals while the team followed them individually with their crafts. About thirty minutes later the snares drop at a scene in the desert where hundreds of war humanoids come out from beneath a tunnel in the ground. The crew watches the visuals on board their crafts, terrified, and in disbelief.

"Holy, Toledo!" Harry gasped.

"Looks like we have more than what we bargained for," Mark said.

"Bargain you say? This is no bargain; this is suicide," Brian remarked.

"I must say, I stand in amazement yet paralyzed by our inconsistency."

He then shakes his head.

Still feeling unsatisfied, Brian walks over to his machine and prepares to transform into a flying craft when suddenly, an enemy warcraft operated by a humanoid quickly attacks him from behind, but he is alerted and dodges the attack while still on the ground.

"Wow, did you see that thing? It came out of nowhere," Brian professed.

"Let's get rid of them," Mark ordered.

The team boarded their machines, and quickly transformed them, enabling them to fly. Once airborne, they locked their targets on the humanoids and opened fire upon them.

At the same time, high above, a spaceship floats in the stratosphere. Inside, Nate is developing plans to take control of the world.

He grins as he walks through the door into the laboratory.

"The time is now, so let's get it done," he said while walking over to a table where a delicate experiment was in progress.

*   *   *   *   *

Meanwhile, Mark and his team battled the humanoid army.

"We're going to need the help of the United States Armed Forces for this," he confessed.

"I agree, cover me I have a plan," Harry suggested.

He then skillfully flew his craft over the humanoid army and dropped an explosive; then maneuvered out and up into the sky as the blast ripped the humanoids apart; at the same time the enemy machines exploded.

"They don't teach you that in the air force," Harry bragged.

Mark continued to battle various machines in the air and was surprised to see Harry.

"Thanks for the cover my man. I can always depend on you," Mark messaged Harry.

"You know I always have your back buddy!"

*   *   *   *   *

In the stratosphere, Nate examines a test tube with human bodies inside. His goal is to take information out of the minds of humans and insert human thought settings into humanoids.

"Well, genetic engineering has brought us a long way and now it's time to take it even further with my design of genetically engineered humanoids, my plan will be unstoppable," he rejoiced.

"But Nate, what will we do with her?" Ricardo says as he looks at Nina lying on the surgical table.

"Send them a message."

*   *   *   *   *

Domonic awakes and removes the accident foam from his body. His eyes slowly roam his surroundings as he makes every effort to become familiar with the environment around him. He stops and looks at Ashley.

"Finally you are awake."

"What happened?" he asked.

"Nate stole the novaerium."

"Novaerium? What is novaerium?"

"The substance, which Mark discovered, is in Nate's hands and he wants to use it to take control of the world," Ashley replied frantically.

Domonic turns to see the live action taking place on screen.

"Looks like my brother is going to need our help," he quoted.

"True, but I don't think it's a good Idea for you to go out there like this."

"Well, just so you know this would be the perfect time, but before we go, help me get this hidden chip out of my system."

Ashley gives Domonic a look of uncertainty before triggering the machine to perform the nano surgery to remove the chip.

* * * * *

It didn't take Domonic and Ashley long to complete the dangerous nano removal-operation and then transform their machine into a refurbished flying jet. Once completed, Domonic locates the battle area and quickly teleports off to the battlegrounds to join the fight. Minutes later they arrived.

"Well, what do you know? Look who's back from the dead," Mark says emphatically.

Suddenly, a craft falling from the sky heads straight for Ashley and Domonic. Mark looks up just in time to warn them.

"Look out!" he yells.

Quickly, Domonic dodged the impending danger of being crushed.

Without hesitation they jump back into their defensive fighting positions to join Mark in combating the enemy.

"I'll shoot from the rear section," Ashley insisted as she moved into position.

She shifts her chair and begins shooting and destroying machines left and right. Without warning, a rare and suspicious damaged craft that seems to have escaped a brutal attack smokes and crash lands out of nowhere. Minutes later a woman exits the craft, staggers a few meters, and while taking off her helmet - falls to

the ground. Harry runs over and investigates and is surprised to find what appears to be his Nina, but little does he know she is a clone.

"What have they done to you? Let me get you inside."

He then tries to communicate with the team but there seems to be no connection.

"Guys, listen, I found Nina and she is alive."

As Harry's craft lifts off a machine fires at him, hitting it on the edge. Within minutes a massive explosion engulfs the area as the battle continues. All the while Nate can see the action taking place on a huge screen inside of his laboratory aboard his spacecraft.

"Not bad for a motley team."

He grins as he walks back to the experimental laboratory.

*   *   *   *   *

"Harry, come in, come in…I think we've lost him," Mark says disappointedly.

Suddenly, Harry's craft twirled out of control and crashes. Nina is unconscious and he tries to wake her.

"Honey are you okay?"

She doesn't answer.

He carefully picks her up and exits the craft and finds a comfortable place to gently lie her down. He then tries sending a message to his team.

"Come in guys, can anyone hear me?"

Unable to get through to anyone, he decides to rest for a while.

Unexpectedly, out in the distant Mark notices an entourage of soldiers coming in his direction.

"Hey look! Our forces will soon multiply," he says excitingly as he watches the arrival of allied troops from the United States Armed Forces.

"What do we do now?' Domonic asks.

"I know Harry is still out there, so let's find him and then continue our pursuit of Nate," Mark replied.

CHAPTER 14

SEARCH AND DESTROY

As the US Armed Forces arrive and Mark's team moves out, a bloody battle begins with Nate's powerful humanoid army. The bright desert sand turned into a sea of blood rocks as armed machinery and chemical defence training soldiers from both sides of the fence move in closer to their targets.

Never has there been such great use of nerve agents designed to immobilize. So intense was the battle that the United Nations called for a cease-fire but to no avail. This was a different era in time and each side had much to gain and plenty to lose.

Clamming with blood, sweat, and tears, the stealth forces experienced an oppressive feeling of pain, yet they continued to destroy their enemy and fight to the death.

The unbearable heat forced Harry and the cloned Nina to seek an underground refuge where they could rest for the night. Harry is still unaware of her biomechanical makeover and continues to treat her as if she was his human love interest.

"I missed you and thought about you often," he said as he attempted to caress her.

"And I missed you too," she says but reluctantly pulls in another direction.

Outside a bomb explodes nearby but it doesn't disturb Harry from noticing Nina's repulsive behaviour and questions it.

"Hmmm, you've changed, what's wrong?" he asks.

"Changed? How so?"

"You almost ripped my arm out."

"Oh, I'm sorry. My mind was on how afraid I was, but now I feel safe in your arms," she conceded somewhat nonchalantly.

Harry had no choice but to accept her feelings. Nevertheless, Nina innocently found her way back into his arms and they later fell asleep.

Night had fallen over the seemingly endless desert as thunder clapped the dark sky. The dry scorching heat of the day was conceded by the coolness of night. Lightning continuously flickered like gigantic fireworks. In the meanwhile, Mark and his team continued to search hoping to get a signal or at least find Harry. They searched until they came across the wreckage of Harry's craft, but still no sign of him. They were not willing to concede that all was lost. They held onto their hopes of finding Harry alive and well.

"Okay team let's call it a night and get some rest. We'll resume first thing in the morning," Mark said.

Unable to settle for finding just the craft, Domonic thinks differently and wants to continue with the search.

"He has to be around here somewhere; I'll do a few more rounds," he says not wanting to concede his anxiety.

"I don't think that would be a good idea because it's too dark and who knows what danger lurks out there," Mark admitted.

"I was going to say the same thing because we don't want to lose anyone else," Brian said agreeably.

Domonic detached his suit from the craft, taking only the portable part, which enables him to activate a light as bright as day.

"Don't worry, I'm on top of this," he says clenching his fist.

"Are you sure? Looks like you could use a little help," Ashley said before following in behind them.

"Sure, come on. I'll welcome the company."

Ashley looked over towards Brian and Mark, before turning to follow Domonic.

"Good luck."

"Alright, call us if you see anything interesting," Brian added.

*   *   *   *   *

Throughout the night and way into the early morning hours Nate inquisitively listens in on Harry and Nina's conversation but after realizing he is listening she immediately turns the device off.

"Why hasn't she killed him yet? What is she waiting for?" Nate mutters to himself.

Chase sits close by, grimacing like a *Cheshire* cat. He rises from his chair and walks over to Nate, drops to one knee, and lowers his head. He then lifts his head and looks at him, making sure to avoid direct eye contact for fear of being thrown into prison or severely punished.

"Nate, I'm thirsty and would be more than happy for a kill."

"A kill?" Nate asked.

"This will be more than a kill. It would be the beginning of the end of civilization on Earth."

Chase tried to understand the logic behind Nate's reasoning but didn't want to fall to contempt.

"This appears to be very important to you," he added.

Nate looked away from Chase momentarily before turning back and grimacing.

"You have no idea."

"And what will I get out of it by completing this task?"

Nate turned and angrily looked at Chase.

"How dare you question me about rewards," he badgered as he raised his neuro-disruptor to strike Chase.

"I thought we had already discussed this, I'm not going to tolerate this type of insubordination, never! ever!"
Nate released a charge from his neuro-disruptor.

Chase backed up and tried to move away but the laser pierced his right middle finger causing it to drop from his hand onto the floor. There was no blood only a finger, wriggling like a worm as its last bit of life is exhausted. Then it stood still, lying there as if it were frozen. Chase picked it up and positioned it back onto his artificial hand.

"I'm sorry sir, please forgive me," he cowered in pain.

Nate stood over the impish little fiend and raised his powerful leg; his booted foot rose above Chase's head preparing to strike.

"If you ever again ask me anything pertaining to your duties, I will squash you like a pea."

He could have stricken Chase and destroyed him if he wanted to, but he decided to allow him to survive this ordeal.

Nate walked away slowly. He had no fear of anything, and it showed. He gave the impression that he was on top of the world and he was - at least for the moment.

"I need you to do me one favour," Nate growled.

"I need you to find Mark and his crew and destroy them."

Chase looked at Nate with slanted eyes. He began to grimace again as he rose to his feet.

"Let it be written," Nate commanded.

Chase then replied, "It will be done."

"And Chase, by the way, see to it that Ricardo gets you an upgrade before leaving on your mission."

Listening all the while, Ryan finds this to be an opportunity for him to prove his worth by teaming up with Chase on this mission.

"I hope you don't mind sharing some of the action tough guy because I'll be joining you," Ryan said enthusiastically.

"And don't you two come back here without my prisoners," Nate said.

Ryan and Chase deploy in separate crafts headed towards Earth to find and destroy their targets. Meanwhile, Mark and Brian rest in their crafts as Ryan and Chase enter Earth's atmosphere with targets locked onto Nina.

The extraordinary thing about being a genetically enhanced humanoid is that programming allows you to experience perception even while in sleep mode; regardless of the fact, she senses danger as it approaches. She becomes tense and shows signs of nervousness. Suddenly, she looks up and appears to be startled by something; and even through the layers of the underground dune, she senses an enemy craft entering Earth's atmosphere. She looks over towards Harry who is fast asleep. This gives her an opportunity to slip out to better inspect the approaching craft. She exits the dune to get a better view of the approaching enemy.

"Oh, man, this is not good," she says.

Chase and Ryan's spacecraft lands about sixty yards from the humanoid replica of Nina. Without their knowledge, she deactivates her tracker allowing her to move through the desert undetected. She then approaches both crafts and disables their computers. Not far off in the distance, Domonic sees the landing and thought it might have been Mark and Brian.

"Glad to see you fellows could join us; what took you so long?" Domonic says in a message sent through his earpiece.

"They must have picked up something," Ashley suggests.

Mark hears the message and replies from his post.

"What are you guys talking about? What's going on out there?"

By this time, it was too late. Domonic and Ashley have already been spotted by Chase and Ryan.

"Chase, do you see what I see?"

Chase is focused on keeping track of the signal then suddenly loses it.

"Damn it, I lost her signal; it was here."

"Forget her for now. We'll take care of her later. In the meantime, let's take care of these two."

The desert is illuminated by the firing of laser beams as Domonic jumps into action, activates his night vision, and returns the fire.

"Get down," Domonic tells Ashley.

While all of this is taking place, Mark listens in through the earpiece.

"You two get out of there, we're on our way," he relays in a message.

Domonic quickly jumps into action. Ashley does the same.

Meanwhile, Mark prepares himself and the craft to head out there. He begins by sending a message to Brian, who is supposedly still asleep in his craft.

"Brian, wake up. Domonic and Ashley are in big trouble, we have to go out there and help them," he says frantically.

Brian, still drowsy from sleep, hears the message through his earpiece and suddenly comes to life and is ready for action.

"What in bloody hell is going on?" he asks.

"Domonic and Ashley seem to be in big trouble; come on let's go," Mark tells him.

They both quickly prepare their crafts to take off and in a matter of seconds they're both airborne and headed out.

Domonic continues to battle with Chase as they fire upon one another. The onset of the night made visibility difficult, but both sides found themselves trapped in a bloody stalemate where neither was able to escape. Ashley then begins firing, hitting Chase but Ryan targets her and takes her out damaging her suit.

"Finish him," Ryan commands.

With the lights out, Mark invisibly manoeuvres his craft within striking distance of the enemy.

Suddenly, without warning he hits them both with his craft, sending them flying along with pieces of their suits falling apart.

"Are you guys alright down there?" Mark asked.

Domonic gets up slowly while Ashley lies still in the sand.

"Hang on; I'm coming to get you," Brian states as he hovers above the desert sand.

Inside the dune, Harry and Nina discuss plans to protect themselves in case of an enemy attack.

"You heard that?" Harry asked.

"Heard what?" Nina replies.

Harry rises to his feet and listens attentively.

"Wait here and stay inside," he says turning to her before heading out of the dune to check the activity.

As he exits, he is confronted with a dust storm.

The storm obscures Harry's vision to the point that he doesn't realize that Nina followed him out. He turns around and barely sees her.

"I said to stay inside. It's dangerous out here."

Nina turns and slowly walks away but turns around once Harry's back is towards her.

Meticulously, he walks towards the dune and stands atop of it, while Nina comes up and stands behind him. He slightly turns and notices her presence.

"Get back inside I tell you."

About a few yards in front of him, Harry notices Brian's shining light from his craft. He appears to be trying to help Domonic, but Chase fires a missile at the craft from his humanoid body. Mark quickly intercepts with laser beams from his neuro-disruptors causing a big explosion.

The shock waves send Brian's craft spinning out of control over the desert. It alerts him to danger as he tries to gain control of it. Domonic finally gets up and targets Chase, firing lasers that eventually dismantles him.

Domonic and Ashley board Brian's craft and sit in the back seat ready to do battle with the enemy forces.

It wasn't long before Harry realizes that it's his teammates fighting the enemy out there.

"Hey, hey, over here," Harry waved his hands and shouted hoping that he could be located.

* * * * *

The dust storm seemed to have grown worse and visibility was eclipsed.

With the infrared system activated, Mark picks up Harry's location with the floodlights of his craft.

"Harry, you crazy, wonderful guy, you're alive," Mark says ecstatically over his machine's speaker system.

Suddenly, Ryan jumps onto Marks craft and lights it up with shots, but Mark quickly activates an electric shield which sends Ryan flying to the ground. Mark then hovers his craft just a few meters off the ground as he beckons Harry to get in.

"I can't leave Nina. She's alone inside the dune. I have to go back and get her."

But what Harry doesn't realize is that while he is away, Nina exits the dune and goes off to help injured Ryan without being detected.

As she approaches, she begins to scold him.

"What are you doing here? I had all this under control, but you ruined it."

Ryan pulls his neuro-disruptor to shoot but she grabs the gun and points it to one side as it fires into the air.

"Leave this to me, now you get out of here," she says forcefully.

She then gives Ryan the chip to his craft that she had removed earlier and quickly leaves.

By the time Harry approached the underground area of the dune, Nina had already returned and was comfortably waiting for him.

"Come on, let's go," he urged.

They both quickly head towards the craft, which was covered in sand. With his bare hands, Harry brushes most of the sand off the top and sides of the machine. He then brushes off the windows and opens the doors. They quickly enter and without hesitation, they take off.

As the craft ascends, the laws of thermodynamics combine with the remaining falling sand, thus producing a shimmering rainbow for all to see.

Ryan watches from an area before he contacts Nate with the news.

"Chase is dismantled, and they have the girl," Ryan claimed.

"What? And you?" Nate asked angrily.

"I could live with it, but I'm going to need some backup."

"Destroy them!" Nate demanded.

Ryan gets up and heads towards his craft. He then inserts the chip which enables the craft to fly again.

*   *   *   *   *

The air was dry and sand dunes were constantly being created by the winds as Brian and Mark's crafts manoeuvred over the desert. It was a huge landscape with mountainous terrain like that of the Himalayas.

"Glad to have you both back. We searched all evening but couldn't get a signal from you," Mark explained as he focused on controlling and executing manoeuvres over the terrain.

"My suit went out when the craft went down. I tried to patch through a signal, but nothing came through," Harry stated.

Meghan finally awoke from a long rest to find the craft on autopilot and Mark looking over her. She yawned and smiled and that was a good sign.

"Hello, sleeping beauty."

"How long have I been asleep?"

"You've been asleep long enough to rejuvenate and that's what's important."

"Wow, I'm speechless."

"How are you feeling?"

"Fine"

"That's my girl"

"No need to worry about me. We have to worry about Nate and his evil plans to take control of the universe."

Mark and Brian's craft flew side by side, giving them the visibility to see each other from the neon green cockpit. Mark then communicates from the earpiece to Brian.

"Are you okay over there?"

"Just a little minor damage but I'm okay."

Brian speaks over his earpiece to Domonic and Ashley, who are just sitting in the back seat of the craft.

"Are you guys alright?"

"We're fine."

"In the words of Lt. John Powers, we're A-Okay," Domonic replies.

"Thank God for these suits. My craft should be just over there."

Suddenly, Brian and Mark's display screen lights up with a warning of incoming danger. Out of nowhere Ryan fires at them, but miraculously they both managed to avoid the danger. Ryan then manoeuvres through the air before firing again and disabling them with missiles.

Upon seeing the destruction exuded by Ryan, Mark becomes filled with anguish.

"Oh no, two crafts down, that's not good."

"What do we do now?" Meghan asked.

"We continue to fight. If we have oxygen in our bodies, a flying craft, and protective suits, we'll be okay."

With the team now crippled by the destruction of two crafts, Mark suggests that the remaining two should be combined into one durable strong machine. After communicating with Brian regarding this, they both land their machines and start the process of fusing the two remaining crafts. Almost immediately, they fuse, changing its concept to a more practical design with the ability to produce even greater performance. It can now host seven crew members seated with their specific task at hand.

"We must find Nate and quickly. We're almost in dire straits so we better act fast," Mark declared.

"And just how are we going to do that?" Harry asked.

"I know where to find him," Nina inserted.

"You do, where?"

She looked up, into the sky, at the forbidden star with a red glow.

"Up there; he is above the world."

"You mean out there in space?"

"Yes, out there far away."

"But how do you know this information?"

"While I was resting in the tube, I saw his plans to go into outer-space as he demonstrated it on the hologram. It showed Mars as his destination."

Mark looked confused but realized that he had to take
on all leads.

"Mars?" he asked curiously.

He pondered for a few seconds then continued.

"The one place I should've thought of," he replied.

Mark gave a command and the team's crafts quickly switched over to intergalactic travel mode. With the power of the Nova, preparation would be a breeze. Mark knew that to prepare for this journey he had to make sure that all the essentials for conducting a space mission of this magnitude were put into place. Intravehicular pressure suits were automatically reinforced to protect each crew member in outer space. Most importantly, he had to make sure he had the manpower and hardware for the electrolysis of water to generate oxygen, along with an ample food supply.

*   *   *   *   *

As they sped off into space, they go into stealth mode where they encounter a variety of spy and warcraft floating above the Earth as if they had no purpose or direction. It was as if they were lost in space. Mark was surprised to see the numerous intergalactic war machines hovering above the Earth, and in no time, the team is already being fired upon. With the intergalactic force field protecting them, they were able to manoeuvre through to their destiny.

*   *   *   *   *

The universe looked stunning as Mark and his team glided through space. As they continued to search for Nate's signal other satellite signals interfered with them making a connection.

They finally radar in on Nate's prime ship as it majestically glided through space. They contemplate whether to launch an all-out full

196

attack before realizing that it's far too large for them to do any external damage.

"I have an idea," Nina suggested.

"What is it?" Mark asked.

"I suggest we create a diversion, manoeuvre as close to the dock, use our invisible shield and when they open the doors, we enter unnoticed by their radars."

"What a wonderful idea. No time to lose. Let's go with it."

Nina takes control of the craft and skillfully manoeuvres it into the dock of Nate's ship as one of his crafts exits.

She then explains the plans to the rest of the crew.

"The command centre is part of a combination space station and floating spaceship, consisting of three parts; the back part is called the dock. It allows other spacecraft of its kind to land and port there. The middle section consists of laboratories, extra rooms for sleeping and relaxing. The front division is called the command centre because it is where all the controls are located. It carries a force field, which protects it. This spaceship is among Nate's prize possessions."

"And you learned all of this when you were encapsulated within the test tube?" Mark asked.

"Even though I appeared to have been in suspended animation, I was still conscious and able to take in the communications around me," Nina replied.

*   *   *   *   *

As the ship floats through the realms of space, Nate is aboard, conducting business between his laboratory and the control board of the command centre along with his lieutenant Arianna, his technical assistant Gunther, and his crew.

Arianna has learned how important it is to be on top of all that is taking place around the galaxy and even on all parts of the ship. Gunther's position is information technology: to work on any technicalities that might arise with the machinery on this sinister vessel.

"We have a signal that an unidentified object of some sort has entered into our doc," Arianna expressed with a sense of urgency.

"Identify it," Nate demands.

"Sending humanoids to investigate," Arianna replies.

She puts a signal through to the humanoid security forces to report to the dock to investigate the unidentified object.

Immediately a humanoid officer secured the dock area and commenced to investigate the visiting spacecraft.

Aboard the ship were Mark, his team and Nina, who navigated their craft skillfully enough to unnoticeably sneak into the doc. But now that they were inside, Mark knew that they must act quickly if they were going to complete their attempt at taking control of Nate's ship.

As they quickly exit their craft to gain supplies, they are fully aware that they are now under surveillance and their cover is exposed.

"Hmmm, the roving eyes of cameras seem to be all over this place. We have to do something about that," Brian pointed out.

He quickly pulled out his plasma gun and shoots the security cameras. Suddenly a warning flares out from the public-address system and is heard all over the ship.

"Intruder alert, intruder alert, intruder alert."

"That didn't work so well; Hurry! We don't have much time," Nina states.

"While they exit the ship, the humanoids attack from all directions sparking a prelude to a battle in outer space in which Mark and his crew would fight incredibly hard. However, Nate planned to take them down and salvage their broken bodies, insert technology and add them to his alien humanoid race.

Arianna watched her screen from the ship's command room.

"Nina is back, and she seems to have company. I don't understand," Arianna exclaims.

In the dock of Nate's ship, the team is surrounded by humanoids as they try and fight their way out of this circle of death.

"They have us surrounded," Meghan said dreadfully.

"What do we do now?" Domonic asked.

As the suspense builds the team has no other choice but to try and get out of this by pushing back the wall of humanoids.

It wasn't long before the team enters the second floor after using the lift. They are faced with a throng of humanoids and only Nina knows the way to the executive space level where Nate is located.

"Follow me," she commanded.

Nina begins to run slowly then with accurate acrobatic sequence, she systematically unlocks a pattern on the ground that opens a vacuum.

"This vacuum will take us up to the top floor of the command centre. Quickly, follow me" Nina shouted before jumping into the vacuum tube.

"I hope she knows where she's going," Brian remarked.

*　　*　　*　　*　　*

Brian, Harry, Meghan, and Ashley hold off the humanoids as they individually enter the tube leading up to the command centre.

"Go, we will handle this!" Harry says pointing to each team member in a sequenced command.

Nina pops out the vacuum of the command centre and walks away, simultaneously changing her appearance and exposing her humanoid features.

"They are all here, all yours now have fun," Nina confirmed.

Suddenly, Mark pops out of the vacuum transport
hitting the floor face down with little time to defend himself. A rather large humanoid in the room quickly grabs him but not before he tries to warn Domonic, but it was already too late and Domonic pops out of the vacuum transport, sliding to one end of the room noticing that it's a trap with little time to defend himself. He fires his laser destroying several humanoids and tried to stun Nina but instead a huge humanoid intercepts his fire, while another knocks him out unconscious. The humanoid then picks him up, along with Mark and uses a magnetic hanger that carries an electric shock to hold and pin them both together. Soon afterwards, Nate walks in to see Mark and Domonic hanging by their suits with the magnetic hanger.

"I must say it's a pleasure to join you this evening my good friends," Nate admitted fascinated by the vision before him.

"You despicable creature you!" Mark yells in anger.

"Someone doesn't seem to be enjoying their visit; could it be that your suit is too tight or maybe the atmosphere doesn't suit you because we can arrange to get you a strait jacket if that's what it'll take to keep your big mouth shut," Nate sneered.

Mark slowly turned his head and looked at Domonic hanging there beside him and on the verge of becoming unconscious.

"Come on, stay here with me buddy," Mark whispered.

"Perhaps a little shock would help," Nate suggested before executing an electric charge to both Domonic and Mark as they both cry out in pain from the electronic jolts.

Meanwhile, on the second floor, the other members of Mark's team battle with the humanoids from different angles. The humanoids begin to attack unaware that Harry has set up a minefield. Just as they reach a certain point, the sensor triggers a bomb which explodes sending them flying with a shock that rattles the entire ship.

"Come on you lousy humanoids," Harry boasted.

He then runs over to an exit area, holds the escape door open while Meghan skillfully uses mixed martial arts to take out a group of the humanoids before becoming invisible.

Unnoticeable, she leaves a ticking bomb amid them which explodes seconds after she exits.

CHAPTER 15

UNEXPECTED GUESTS

Mark was continuously tortured with the electric shock-waves executed by Nate and he cried out in terrible pain. During this time, without warning, another explosion rattles the ship. Nate signalled the humanoids to take Mark and Domonic to the holding cell but on second thought - changes his mind telling them to leave Mark behind.

"There is something special I have in mind for this one," he said defiantly.

He then looked up at Mark hanging there helplessly strapped to a metal frame with both hands extended out and his face pointed to the ground.

"Jesus couldn't have done it any better. Whoever says he who abides in him ought to walk in the same path in which he did, well I think you're about to do a fine job, my friend."

Mark was dumbfounded and didn't utter a word but just looked down precariously at Nate.

In the ships dock, the humanoids carefully inspected Mark's craft and discovered Ruth on board. While all of this was taking place, Domonic was strapped to a metal frame and hanging in the holding cell, stripped of his suit except for its skin layer.

As a security precaution, a humanoid approached the table to inspect Domonic's disposition. Domonic plays as if he is weak and not able to move a muscle but as soon as the humanoid turns his back and walks away he raises and thrust his legs forward, hooking both around the humanoid's thick neck to strangle it.

The humanoid screamed in terror. It suffers slight immobility but was able to get his hands on his weapon and fire laser beams wildly, missing Domonic's head by a few centimetres various times; but instead, the blast hits and destroys the chains holding him, allowing both Mark and Domonic to drop to the ground.

Domonic skillfully rolls to one side with the humanoid firmly gripped to his feet and slams it hard against the wall. He then flips up off the ground releasing his arms from behind him and as the humanoid readies itself, Domonic grabs the chains still hanging, hooks the humanoid's feet together turning it upside down and dismantles it by kicking it into the wall. He then uses the humanoid's laser to cut himself loose before arming himself.

As he exits the cell he is faced with more humanoids, which he eliminates with mixed martial arts and laser beams as he finds his way back through the ship to attempt to rescue his team.

Swiftly, the rest of the team enters the hallway of the ship but are forced to split up; Meghan and Ashley take one section and Brian and Harry take another, though, throughout the battle, they still manage to communicate with one another.

"If you don't remember anything, always remember what Mark taught us, don't be afraid to use that suit; just think how the suit was designed to always protect you!" Ashley communicated to Harry through her earpiece.

Suddenly, Meghan hears a suspicious sound but doesn't quite know where it's coming from.

"Quiet, listen, do you hear that?" Ashley asked.

They look left and right and then look up to see a strange humanoid in ninja form attacking from the air, coming down upon them like an eagle about to pounce upon its prey, but it was already too late to avoid this unexpected attack.

Meghan is slashed and bleeding but is soon back on her feet and turns invisible to counterattack but is quickly stopped by the ninja humanoid's calculated moves. It picks her up and holds her in the air with one hand before preparing to annihilate her.

With a few flips, Ashley is back on her feet and heads straight towards her opponent before performing a flying side kick explicitly meant to wreck it, but the anthropomorphic creature has already figured her moves and knocks her clear out of the air with one thrust of its metallic forearm.

Meghan then uses both arms to slam the sides of the humanoid ninja's head, executing a rounded side kick into its chest before performing a somersault and landing on her feet with the precision of a cat. She then becomes airborne, twisting herself to avoid being attacked, as she passes the dazed ninja humanoid; finally landing in position aside Ashley.

At this moment Meghan and Ashley realize that if they are going to defeat this powerful ninja they will have to team up and utilize their specialized skills. Together, they coordinate a strategy which results in them both crushing the ninja.

"You haven't seen the last of me," the defeated ninja humanoid promised as it vanishes leaving only a puff of blue smoke behind.

"I didn't know ninjas speak," Ashley said inquisitively.

"Neither did I. Clearly, this one speaks quite well, which is unusual."

"Wait a minute; there was something familiar about its voice."

"What do you mean?" Meghan asked.

"Didn't it sound like Nina?"

"Well, there's only one way to find out," Meghan replied.

"Let's plug into our radio frequency identifier and see if we can pick up where it disappeared to."

As Meghan and Ashley continue their pursuit, Brian and Harry outline their strategy to find Mark as quickly as possible.

"You take that side of the ship and I'll take this side, and remember, in case of an emergency, we'll communicate through our earpiece," Harry commanded.

With great fortitude, Harry was always prepared to take on the role of leader if in the event Mark was unable to fulfil his duties. He had already discussed the possibility of leadership with Mark and Meghan. He knew that Mark trusted him, and their loyalty went as far back as from the time when they were children. Brian knew this and therefore, he followed his commands effortlessly.

"Sounds good mate," he replied.

*　*　*　*　*

The dimly lit corridors of the ship made an ideal cover for Harry and Brian as they continued to fight their way through it in search of Mark. There seemed to be many perils and obstacles surrounding them, but their mission was to succeed. Harry was fearless, a good fighter, and very courageous. Brian was a true soldier and would do whatever it took to accomplish a goal, especially when it came to his teammates.

Meanwhile, in another area of the ship, Ryan and Domonic engage in full battle. Brian hears their confrontation in the ships rat-infested boiler room and goes to investigate. He encounters the gladiators engaged in full battle as giant space rats run aimlessly attempting to escape the titans. But it appears that Ryan has Domonic down for the count and Brian is forced to save him.

He stabilizes himself and fires a cable onto Ryan then quickly places it on the wall. This action slings him backwards with great force. Ryan quickly fires back at Brian as he crosses to help Domonic but misses, instead blowing some pipelines forcing Brian to jump to the other side as they explode.

Brian finally rescues Domonic and quickly departs the area. But, then something catches his attention. He looks down at his forearm device and notices his suit percentage is dangerously low due to the configuration of the novaerium's use by Nate inside the spaceship. He knows that for his suit to operate properly, it must be fully charged. Because of this, Brian is forced to take off his suit to sustain mobility otherwise it would harden and encapsulate him, thus restricting his movements. Nevertheless, he is still able to transform his suit into an upper body armour vest.

Unexpectedly, Ryan appears after exiting the steamy boiler room and seems to be searching for his opponents. Brian notices him and fires his weapon. Ryan returns the fire from an angle and Domonic intervenes from another angle, hitting and knocking him unconscious.

Domonic then turns towards Brian and notices that he is hurt. He looks down at the bloody mess on the floor of the ship and shakes his head.

"Are you okay? You're hit!"

"It's nothing. I'll be okay," Brian admitted but then suddenly falls to the ground in a resting position.

"Come on, I have you," Domonic asserted as he quickly helps Brian up by supporting him on his shoulder. They enter the lift going up, but Ryan appears out of nowhere and runs towards the lift and fires at it just before it closes.

"Damn it!" he mutters to himself.

"I better let Nate know about the unexpected guests coming in his direction."

*   *   *   *   *

After Ruth's revival, she and Nate enter the laboratory to check on Ricardo's progress. He is in the process of adding organic and bio-mechatronic body parts to compliment the already placed genetic enhancing features of an experiment he was working on which involved cloning world leaders.

"How much longer is this process going to take?" Nate asked.

"They are just about ready," Ricardo replied.

"That's not good enough for me. I repeat, how much longer is the process going to take?"

Ricardo turns the computer screen around and shows Nate the progress report.

"Alright, that looks good. We must hurry!" Nate says demandingly.

Nate and Ruth quickly rush out of the laboratory leaving Ricardo behind to complete his project. As they travel through the corridor of the ship, they encounter Nina making her way toward the laboratory.

While all of this is taking place, Harry secretly plants a minefield, placing sensor type bombs in various areas of the ship and incapacitating a few humanoids in the process.

From a distance Harry observes Nina entering through a secret door that opened into Nate's laboratory. Curiosity gets the best of him and he decides to activate his invisible shield so that he can watch Nina's entrance inconspicuously. After the doors close, he quickly looks for a platform where he could observe the inside of the laboratory.

Harry soon disables his invisible shield and looks inside through a small high-level window where he sees Ricardo, the cloned Nina, his girlfriend Nina, and the humanoid world leaders. He is surprised at the entire operation taking place; even the site of the cloned Nina as she instantly changes her appearance.

What in the universe is going on here? Harry wonders to himself, quite confused.

Without warning, the alarm goes off and a robotic voice announces, "Intruder alert, intruder alert, intruder alert."

*　　*　　*　　*　　*

In the meantime, while all of this is taking place, Ricardo and Nina can see everything on surveillance cameras located outside. They observe closely as Harry runs for cover.

"Stop him; he must have seen the whole operation. It's time!"

Ricardo confirms and then presses a button which releases armed cloned humanoid world leaders aboard a satellite to Earth on a mission to destroy the planet. Harry is shocked at what he just witnessed and is not sure what to do. He tries to catch his breath as he communicates from his earpiece to the rest of the team.

"Guys, there appears to be something quite unusual going on in the...!"

Before he finishes his sentence, he is stunned by a humanoid and captured.

It appears to be a horrible situation as Ricardo now holds Harry hostage in a laboratory room strapped to a gurney and is attempting to clone him.

"I was wondering when you were going to arrive to try and rescue your little girlfriend then attempt to run out of here like a hero," Ricardo retorted.

"What kind of bloody mess is this?" Harry questioned.

"If you came a little earlier I would have shown you exactly what it is but now it's too late. You see her?" Ricardo said as he points to Nina.

Harry struggles to break loose.

"My creation standing over there is what made your heart all fluttery," Ricardo articulated.

"I should've known you weren't real. You tricked us into outer space."

Harry yields as he stares at the cloned Nina standing inside the room.

Harry's real girlfriend, Nina, who is lying on the table, awakes but keeps her eyes closed after hearing the conversation. Ricardo then prepares Harry for cloning while he keys the instructions into the computer.

"Well, since you're not such a great fighter I'm going to have to make you into a better one," Ricardo arranged.

"What?" Harry responds.

He wrestles with the straps on the machine as it sends an electric shock slightly stunning him. Nina lies on the table with electrodes connected to her body, while she calmly anticipates the opportunity to escape. With quick thinking, Nina's up and off the table like the matrix attacking her replica.

"Take this you creep; that's for stealing my identity."

Harry notices Nina is alive. Excited he gathers up the energy to somehow manage to knock Ricardo to the side but as he tries to escape a humanoid fires its neuro at him. The laser beams slightly miss killing him by a few centimeters, but instead, the beams slice through the straps of the gurney, enabling him to get his hands free. He quickly escapes the cloning process and then disables the humanoid, taking its neuro-disruptor, then grabbing Nina, before rushing out the door. While exiting, he shoots a chemical component into the laboratory, which explodes causing damage to Ricardo's face, causing him to shout in pain as Harry and Nina escape.

CHAPTER 16

DESTINATION MARS

The atmosphere spelt doom for Mark as he found himself at the mercy of Nate's iniquity. He became a victim of torment as Nate administered electrical shockwaves to try and get information out of him regarding the novaerium. Mark felt a jagging thrust in his thighs and back and then both his legs started to become weak. It appeared as if the ground became closer as he became dazed by the tortuous shockwaves.

In the process, Nate observed Mark continuously before executing more high voltage shockwaves in trying to get him to talk.

"Wake up, you're missing all the fun. After all, you did come to retrieve what I stole from your laboratory or why else would you have come here?"

"You have no idea what power that source holds," Mark exclaimed.

Nate looked up, turned his head away from Mark and walked a few meters before stopping and looking at his prisoner with an appearance of grandeur. He then took on a repugnant grin letting out a squeal as if he were an animal being butchered to death.

"Oh, I know, believe me I know," he confessed.

Mark tried his best to wiggle out of his bondage but there was no way possible for this to be done. He then cried out to Nate.

"You must let me out of here. For all I know this entire universe could be imploded with the use of the novaerium, you don't know what power you possess in your hands. I demand that you release me" Mark pleaded.

Nate turned to him and grinned.

"Is that so? As far as you can see my entire ship is powered by the novaerium and you say I don't know how to use such source of power? Nonsense! What fools you mortals be," he squawked.

"Think about what you're doing; think about all the precious lives you'll be destroying on Earth," Mark pleaded.

Nate looked at him and turned away. He then pulled up a hologram display blueprint in the open space of the command centre and presented his plan that was already in progress for Mars. He then looked back at Mark and obviously despised him.

"Home you say?"

He then turned around to look through the cockpit of

the ship onto Mars as they approached the red planet.

"This will be my world; say hello to my planet Mars. I will colonize it and create a new kingdom. Think about what we could achieve if we just work together," Nate revealed.

Mark obviously didn't like his ideas and they made him sick to his stomach just trying to fathom them.

"No, you mustn't, no way..." Mark pleaded.

"Yes, there is a way. I am the way. Just imagine all the possibilities when I gain absolute power over the entire universe. I will be the new power in space that will control the Earth and all the other planets and Mars will be my kingdom. There will be no neutron stars coming my way, no destruction, none of that when I become emperor of the universe. All things will change, and the entire galaxy will be all mine!"

Mark couldn't believe his ears and angrily tried to break free but was firmly bounded.

"God help us," he pleaded mercifully.

Nate looked at Mark sympathetically saying "yes, you're right," as he appeared to be speaking from false consensus.

Suddenly, there was a piercing scream from the hall of the ship. For the first time Mark appeared to host fear.

"What the heck are you doing to cause all the chaos on board this ship?"

"Chaos, did you say chaos?" Nate asserted.

"Everything I've done I've kept a record in my head and so I can account for the crime and the punishment. That's something you mortals never claim; you see It's not chaos I'm starting; it's the revitalization of the entire population or what's left after I'm done with it."

Mark looked at Nate discouragingly as he continued.

"I'm attempting to save thirteen billion humans, which includes those isolated that escape the census, from the onslaught of an approaching neutron star. It will destroy the Earth and almost all of mankind."

"This is madness. There's a force field in place to protect the Earth from such an impending danger."

Nate listened but partially ignored Mark as he continued to work on securing some important documents.

Then he turned to Mark and asked a question.

"Does it seem correct to you that one is punished, and another isn't for his crime against humanity? Do you expect those who have committed crimes to move on with the rest of us?"

Mark angrily looked back at Nate.

"There is no need to punish all of mankind for your little experiment, which is bias experimentation. I know your plan and it is not for the betterment of mankind" Mark raged in anger.

"God help us if you are out there," Mark whispered.

He then lowered his head in a praying mode and continued.

"This man must be stopped. I know you wouldn't allow one man to destroy a planet. There must be some evil force behind all of this. God help us."

He then raised his head and looked over at Nate.

"You won't survive out here, it's not safe," Mark said.

"Now don't you worry, I have it all planned, can't you see. I am alpha and omega, the beginning and the end," Nate said as the pupils of his eyes took on a triangular shape and turned a murky green colour.

He then walked away from the command board of the ship, but then quickly stopped in his tracks and turned towards Mark.

"I'll be back."

* * * * *

A silver vapour mysteriously appeared and moved playfully across the floor towards Mark. As if by some sort of magic, a cloud rose out of the abyss and formed an illusionary figure of a goddess with a lion's head and a sun disk and uraeus upon her head.

Mark gasped and turned his head in fear before realizing that he can't hide but must face this new adversary.

"What kind of creature are you?" he asks fearfully.

"I am the goddess Sekhmet. I have been sent by Mars, the god of war to assist you."

"But how did you come to me?" he asked inquisitively.

"The gods have been watching you and your work for a long time. They believe in you and what you are trying to accomplish. They know of your adversary Nate, and how he is trying to defeat your purpose and that is why I've been sent to guide and protect you."

221

As Sekhmet spoke the room became moist and precipitated in some areas. It appeared as if everything was frozen in time. The goddess continued.

"For many centuries I have protected the Sun god Ra who continues to rule the universe. I was informed by the muses that the possibility of war in space is inevitable to see who is powerful enough to take possession of the universe and at the same time, a neutron star is heading towards Earth to destroy it. You must warn the people. You must be the savior of humanity from the probability of massive destruction."

Mark listened attentively and then questioned the goddess about Nate. He was careful not to look straight into her eyes as the illumination around her was overwhelming.

"But how will you help protect me from Nate?"

The goddess waved her hand and what appeared to be a small interstellar cloud rose from the floor as if it were a genie coming out of its lamp. When it cleared there laid a gold embroidered silk pouch. She then roared in a foreign tongue and miraculously Mark fell from his entrapment and landed on his knees unharmed.

"You must quickly pick up this pouch and look inside," she said.

Mark followed her orders. Inside the pouch he found his wooden Kalimba that was left in his laboratory beneath the bar and grill. He gently plucked one of the metallic strings and a tone sounded.

"And what is the meaning of this and how can this help me here?" he asked.

The goddess moved closer towards Mark.

"You must always keep this pouch in your possession and hidden from your enemies. This will be one of your secret powers from here on."

The goddess then continued.

"The ancient instrument inside of the pouch will help protect you and keep you safe."

"But how?"

"When plucked individually, the seven strings will release one of your seven protectors based on your needs, one which will be *Ntwadumayla*, the red dragon of Mars."

"The red dragon of Mars? And then after he protects me can I call on him again?"

"After you are protected, you will be given an apocalypse which will explain your second coming."

"My second coming? Whatever does that mean? I'm not dead."

"No, you're not but Nate had already graduated your doom."

She paused and then turned away from Mark in the direction of the interstellar cloud, which still floated freely. She waved her hand slowly in front of it and a hologram appeared which exposed his future.

"Look," she said as the cloud showed a vision.

Mark peered closer and was able to distinguish himself interchangeably passing through what appeared to be a huge cloud. As he floated freely, out of nowhere a giant humanoid appeared with spikes and clubbed hands. He grabbed Mark and threw him to the ground before raising his giant clawed feet and trampling him. He then raised a sharp javelin and furiously pierced him in the ground. Mark quickly turns away from the vision, holds his head in shame and covers his eyes.

"What must I do now?"

"You must go find your friends and return to Earth. You must leave the atmosphere of Mars. If you decide to stay you must be received by the red dragon, which will protect you from the moment you set foot on Mars throughout the remainder of your time there."

"But it's beyond my powers. Nate is in control here. How can the red dragon protect me from Nate and what kind of powers does he hold?"

In the blink of an eye, Sekhmet vanished into thin air leaving Mark bewildered.

He then looked at the spot where Sekhmet appeared and noticed an illuminated inscription. He moved in to take a closer look. It appeared to be strange writing, like hieroglyphics, which he could not understand.

* * * * *

Domonic and Brian are in the storage room. An unusual place to be but they found it proper to explore and map as much of Nate's ship as possible. In their plan to take over the ship, they wanted to make sure that they knew every intricacy that went into its infrastructure.

"Do you hear that?" Domonic stated.

"What do you have there?" Brian requested.

"A sound, it seems to be coming from over there."

The noise appeared to get louder as if something or someone was trying to get out of a locked position.

Brian keyed in on where the sound was coming from.

"I think I've found it," he said.

He moved closer to listen. Domonic plugged in a device into a machine to override and open the door. The knocking appeared to get louder.

"Hold on, we're coming," Brian shouted in the direction of the sound. The door slowly opened revealing Mark.

"Well, what do you know? Finally, we've found you."

"We must move quickly to stop this ship from landing on Mars."

"What do you mean? What are you talking about?"

"Hey, where are the rest of the team members?"

"They're on board fighting for their lives."

Mark looked worried and then announced, "We must gather them all together. I need to talk with them quickly. The dogmas have changed."

At that moment Nate arrives at the holding cell with two humanoids; one carries a suit for Mark, but their plans quickly change after they realize that Mark had escaped.

Nate is astonished and yells in disbelief.

"Where is the prisoner? Find him quickly before he gets off the ship and bring him to me now."

As the ship prepares to dock on Mars, Mark and some of the members of his crew gather in a secluded section of the ship discussing their next move.

"Damn it. That entire ship is rigged; there must be a way out," Brian answered.

"What do you mean rigged?"

"Harry planted bombs throughout the whole ship while you were captured."

"Where is the rest of the crew?" Mark asked.

"They're trying to find you. The entire ship is set for destruction, so we must move quickly."

Meanwhile, Nate and his humanoid army exit the ship onto Mars station. He is feeling imperial and orders a command. Immediately the humanoids cheer him on as if he were their king. Surrounded by his army, he triumphantly makes his way towards the arena through the pressurized glass transportation terminal connecting it from Mars station.

Still, in hiding aboard the ship, Mark and some members of his crew try to come up with a solution to defeat Nate, overtake his ship, and to return to Earth.

CHAPTER 17

A GIFT FROM A GODDESS

Amidst the potential fate of doom, Mark's team advanced to combat Nate's humanoids as they made attempts to find him. However as the fighting progressed, the colliding forces battled one another using powerful weaponry such as neuro-disruptors, a variable gun with plasma, electromagnetic pulse and other destructive possibilities obtained by just changing the mode.

The crushing forces of the humanoids were invariably seeking to destroy their quarries within the spaceship. The rest of Mark's team was unable to withstand the oppression and withdrew to safety. Withstanding the risk of getting captured or killed, the team remained hidden and used different attack strategies to take out their enemy. There was no room for mistakes and the playing ground was limited inside the mega spaceship docked on Mars station. Occasionally, the team was able to use rounds of electromagnetic pulses to take down a few humanoids, consequently freeing up their capacity to make their way outwards.

Nevertheless, the team endeavoured to remain inconspicuous aboard Nate's ship, only venturing out to assault the army of humanoids that were seeking to catch and destroy them. It was a terrible and deadly battle throughout and though they were outnumbered, they were able to slay a plethora of the humanoids.

In the meantime, Mark sought to signal his team from his space suit, but he didn't realize that his communications signal was weak. The supposedly durable Kevlar material and the technological functions of the suit were nearly destroyed from the electric shocks that were executed by Nate. Even his suit could not protect him from the vengeance of Nate's warfare. However, he focused his energy on utilizing the sudden power of the novaerium to send telepathic messages to his team.

"This is Mark. Can you hear me?"

Nonetheless, as hard as Mark sought to get his message transmitted, there was no acknowledgement whatsoever from any of his team members. It appeared that there wasn't a connection between them. Nevertheless, he continued his messaging.

'We must stop Nate from destroying mankind,' he communicated but still his team did not respond.

Moments after sending the third message, Mark's mutation emits causing his lower extremities to become weak resulting in the floor becoming closer as his legs weakened. The mutation emits an impulse that distorts Mark's imagination, leaving him in a state of suspended animation, pushing his genes to points unknown, increasing his adrenaline flow far beyond its normal capacity. He tries to sustain his equilibrium but is unable to as the major organs of his body become damaged by the secretions of alien chemicals into his bloodstream.

But somehow, he pulls himself across the floor into an area where he is invisible to the sinister humanoids out to capture and destroy him. As he sits inconspicuously on the floor of the spaceship, he thinks back on the very day when this all began, not long ago, when he first encountered the purple chemical oozing out of the meteorite. His subconscious mind reflects when he first saw the meteorite racing across the darkened sky over the mountains of Nanga Parbat; not knowing that in this meteorite there was an alien substance that was encapsulated.

He remembered the moment when the substance precipitated onto his body resulting in a conflict for which he was not quite prepared. He felt that he had to emancipate himself from the mental slavery which was attempting to engulf his mind and take control of his body. His equilibrium seemed to wane, and he had no alternative but to attempt to bolt back. It was his advent moment; however, he wanted so desperately to overcome this whole thing which he did not totally understand.

He continued to try and compose himself, but it was difficult. Time and time again, his mind went back to that moment when he was lying on the ground in the wilderness after making initial contact with the novaerium.

There was a constant beating in his head like someone was pounding a drum. The reality of it all started to reveal itself. Then, without warning, sounds of alien footsteps hammered the floor of the ship.

The symptoms of the mutation overpowered him as he sat helplessly in a corner, fighting to stay conscious and relative to the reality of his surroundings, while holding on to his weapon ready to fire upon any marauders that happened to come his way.

Finally, unable to withstand the pressures, he collapsed to the ground, lying as if he were dead. Though his body was in a frozen state, in his mind, he was able to see the writing on the wall which foretold of his impending doom. Ambiguously, the epitaph and postlude to immortality haunted him, paradoxically, he knew that he was not dead and that he was still very much alive. In his dream state, he visualized a bright light in the abyss of his subconscious.

His mind appeared to roam through space, and he perceived that he had landed at the sight of the fallen meteorite back in Pakistan. He reminisced on the mountainous region of the Himalayas as he rested there on the ground; surely, this was the astonishing scene where the crater was birthed.

It wasn't long before his blurry eyes picked up an illuminated object floating towards him; this time it appeared to shine brighter as if someone was holding it and moving closer. He tried to call out but his weaken muscles had yet to restore enough strength for him to open his mouth. He was able to move his eyes around, but he could not speak.

He then remembered the kalimba given to him by the goddess Sekhmet and reached for the pouch and managed to pluck what sounded like an ancient alien tune. It was at this very moment that he experienced an epiphany.

Suddenly, the light illuminated the entire ship, dissipating the darkness and Mark noticed that he appeared to be floating as if he were in purgatory. Then he heard a mighty cry echo throughout the abyss as the sky darkened as if it were the end of time.

Without warning, a massive tornado spun toward him, beyond him, and then disappeared. Then a comet opened before him and there was a clatter of hoofs as a rider came out from it, revealing a huge golden chariot drawn by seven majestic horses with seven unusual crowns; it was the goddess Sekhmet at the helm.

There was a white horse whose crown was Saturn, whose composition was made of poisonous gases. There was a red horse with a crown of fire, whose body was lava and whose hoofs were like the talons of a mighty eagle; there was a grey horse with a crown of lead and whose body was volcanic ash, a black horse whose body was midnight and whose crown was the hood worn by Death, a golden horse with a golden crown; a vaporous body like the planet Jupiter with the claws, mane, and head of a lion, a silver horse with a jeweled crown of diamonds, rubies, sapphires and whose body was made of mercury with a mane containing one-thousand cobras-hissing and spitting out poison throughout the universe; and yes, these were the one thousand rumor-mongers that spread hypocrisy. And there was a pale green horse called Earth adorning a crown of humility, shame, and suffering, whose cry was that of a child pleading for forgiveness, whose hoofs contained the suffering faces of men crying out for mercy.

From the chariot, Sekhmet looked down upon the helpless Mark. Her eyes glowed with the wisdom of a million years; they burned with the destructive forces of wars - past, present, and future wars, and had the weariness of having travelled through many galaxies. She then moved closer to him.

Finally able to speak, Mark cried out, "What am I doing here? What is happening to me?"

The goddess looked down at the mere mortal lying before her and couldn't help but have a bit of sympathy for him as she spoke to him in a loud voice.

"You are the chosen one. You will be given powers no man will ever know, but you must first learn how to use and control this power."

"But I don't understand" Mark cried out.

Sekhmet hovered even closer to Mark.

"Ten years ago, while you were there on Nanga Parbat, your life was spared by a mighty red dragon that protected you into the night. The dragon let out a mighty roar and it was heard by the gods. It was then you were chosen to regenerate the culture and traditions of the world and be the protector of all humanity" she proclaimed.

"But why me and what is my purpose?"

"You must save the Earth, its ecology and environment. You are the salvation of all humanity and have been chosen by the gods to save the planet and its people."

Mark was perplexed by Sekhmet's message yet had regained a bit of strength and painfully tried to get up from the floor. She then continued.

"By being chosen you have been given gifts that will turn you into a powerful gladiator. Here in your mind is the only place to truly understand and enhance the gifts that the gods have bestowed upon you."

"Then how do I get out of here?" Mark hastily asked.

"In time you will understand that with your powers there is no place in the galaxy that can retain you; there is no place in our universe you cannot go. Only you have the power to control your destiny. Unaware of the hearts and nature of man you have chosen to save them. That will be your destiny."

Sekhmet paused, then rotated her head looking over the four corners of the universe, before turning back to Mark.

"Come whither. I will show you things that will explain the propensity of your newly acquired powers."

Mark boarded the chariot with Sekhmet and they quickly sped away on a journey, through space, back in time, to learn about this divine power that grows within him. It didn't take long for him to realize the salvation of mankind was being placed upon his shoulder, and he was ready to accept this messianic challenge.

As quickly as the journey started, it was soon over. Mark found himself opening his eyes to the same scene left on the spaceship, alone sitting upright in the corner, before passing out.

This time he wasn't gasping for air and he felt much stronger. But just as quickly as he jumped back to reality he was, again, overpowered by some strange hidden force which knocked him unconscious.

After a moment, it became completely dark. When his eyes opened for the third time he felt, again, as if he were in purgatory. He felt as if he was caught between two worlds.

Suddenly, as he looked down at himself, he noticed he had on unfamiliar, shiny garments, like armour.

Mark thought he was imagining and touched himself from the crown of his head down to his ankles to make sure he was still alive. He felt the cloth of his new space suit. He was astonished, having never seen such material, the likes of which now covered his entire body. It was as if he were wearing a second skin, yet his suit was equipped with all the gadgets needed for space travel.

He was amazed as to how he had awakened from a point of no return to a point where he was now more powerful than he's ever been in his entire life and ready to conquer the evil forces of the universe. The astonishing thing was that his new suit was illuminated like stardust in the cosmos.

Mark looked up into the heavens and stretched out his arms on both sides. As he looked up, he noticed that his vision was extraordinary and that he had the power to see straight into the far-reaching areas of the universe.

He was able to see through the walls of the ship as if he had x-ray vision. In his observation, he noticed a new area of the solar system beyond the reaches of Earth with an unusual copper landscape which met his gaze.

His vision was as intelligent as it had ever been, and it appeared that the gods had given him superhuman functions. His other senses; those of hearing, smell, taste, and touch were supreme.

From his platform within the ship, he was able to visualize Olympus Mons, the highest known volcanic mountain in the galaxy. He noticed it in the distance before him even though he had not ever seen it.

Phobos, one of the almost stationary moons hanging in the sky over the punctured valleys of Mars, was visible to him and it appeared that he was able to see right through into its craters and landscape as if he were standing on its surface.

He could barely believe his eyes, but the truth slowly forced itself upon him; he was looking at Mars from the same immaterialism from which ten years earlier he had gazed upon the messenger from Mars; the messenger which brought the purple substance which was inside the meteorite that fell from the sky over Nanga Parbat, 55.957 million kilometers away on planet Earth.

www.ingramcontent.com/pod-product-compliance
Lightning Source LLC
Chambersburg PA
CBHW021147110726
47900CB00002B/469